A GAMBLER'S HEART

Love's A Gamble Book One

KAY P. DAWSON

A Gambler's Heart
Print version
© Copyright 2021 (As Revised) Kay P. Dawson

CKN Christian Publishing
An Imprint of Wolfpack Publishing
5130 S. Fort Apache Rd. 215-380
Las Vegas, NV 89148

www.cknchristianpublishing.com

Print ISBN 978-1-63977-080-9

A GAMBLER'S HEART

CHAPTER 1

"Stop fussing with your dress and lift your eyes up. It's no wonder you've never been able to attract anyone. You're slouched over in the corner where no one can even see you."

Fiona sat perfectly still, reaching her hands out to press against her gown. She knew there weren't actually any wrinkles but it kept her from having to look out at the ballroom.

At her stepmother's words, she lifted her eyes and swallowed the lump in her throat as she took in the sight of the beautiful gowns all around her. They danced in and out of her vision as the men swept the lucky women around in their arms, twirling them around on the dance floor.

This was the third ball she'd been to in the past few days and she'd only had a handful of dances. Even those had only been with some of her father's friends who surely felt sorry for her or men she'd rather not have been dancing with anyway.

She'd had her coming out ball over two years ago, so the only men she was attracting now were the less desirable catches who knew their choices were limited.

Her stepmother had married her father after her mother died five years ago. He was an Irishman living in London and marrying a woman of Viola Dunning's status in society was considered quite an accomplishment.

That is, unless you were unlucky enough to be Fiona or one of her two sisters, Cora and Aileen.

Viola had two of her own daughters who were in the middle of their seasons and both were attracting all the right suitors. The possibilities were endless for the girls as they were courted vigorously by a selection of eligible men.

Cora and Aileen would have their seasons soon and Fiona had no doubt they'd have no trouble attracting matches for themselves. Both of them were beautiful, having inherited their mother's blonde hair that seemed to sparkle and change colors depending on the light.

Fiona was graced with her father's red hair and while it drew attention, it wasn't the kind a woman hoped to attract.

However, it wasn't only her hair that drew people's eyes to Fiona.

She'd been stained or blessed, depending on your point of view, with a red birthmark that stretched from the bottom of her jaw and down her neck. Her mother used to remark that it was in the shape of a heart and was a kiss from heaven.

But Fiona didn't feel that way about it. And it was apparent most other people didn't either.

The birthmark seemed to get redder when she was worried or under stress and the past two years had been full of both. She hadn't ever been prepared for a season in London, until her father had married Viola.

Now Fiona had spent her seasons watching others find suitors and become married while she still sat on the sides watching. She tried not to let it get to her but, the truth was, she was tired of feeling like she wasn't as beautiful as the other girls. She wanted to get as far away from all of this as she could but she didn't know how.

Standing, she held her hands clutched in front of her as she turned to Viola. "I think I will turn in for the night. I'm feeling so tired from the endless balls this week. I will send Miles back after he has dropped me at home." Miles was the family coachman who she knew would be waiting outside.

He would be a welcome face to see.

Her exit from the ballroom went unnoticed, she was sure.

"Good evening, Miss Fiona. Did you have a good

night?" The servants all knew they could be friendly with her as she'd never gotten used to having others wait on her. She treated them all with kindness and they returned it to her.

His warm smile choked her up with emotion. He never looked at her like she was different and Fiona desperately needed to see a friendly smile after the night she'd spent watching everyone else have so much fun.

She smiled warmly at the older man as he held out his hand and took hers to help her into the carriage. "It was fine, Miles." She didn't trust her voice to say anything more.

He simply nodded at her, seeming to understand her need to avoid conversation about the evening. She looked out at the streets of London as they made their way back to the townhouse, watching other carriages go by, the sound of the horse's hooves clip-clopping on the cobblestones.

She missed the country. She wasn't a city girl. When her father had married Viola, they had moved to London, leaving her beloved country home behind.

She much preferred the solitude and the openness of the land. In the countryside, she could go outside and walk around in peace. She didn't have to deal with people who were initially drawn to the beauty of a young woman, quickly averting their eyes when they got close enough to notice the mark on her face. No matter how many times it had happened in her life, it still hurt.

The carriage pulled up to the front and Miles helped her down. She felt him give her gloved hand a gentle squeeze and she lifted her eyes to his.

"You were absolutely stunning tonight, Miss," he whispered the words to her so no one else would be able to overhear. She knew he was taking a risk speaking to her and it lifted her spirits to know he cared enough to take that chance.

She lifted her skirts and moved up the stairs to the house as fast as she could go, ignoring the servants who all bustled to help her as she came through the door. She just needed to get to her room where she could be alone.

Closing the door behind her, she knew it was only a matter of time until she had the maids coming to help her get changed and ready for the night. Something she'd always managed to do on her own up until she'd been forced to move to London.

She sat down at her dressing table, looking in the mirror at the girl staring back at her. Her skin was pale except for cheeks that were slightly flushed from the run up the stairs.

But when she turned her head to the side, she could see the birthmark standing out in bright red contrast to the white of her skin, despite the best efforts of the powder Minnie had applied.

Tears slowly made their way down her cheeks as

she looked into the green eyes that shone with wetness. Why couldn't she be as beautiful as her sisters?

She reached for the small newspaper sticking out from under her table where she'd hidden it. She'd heard other girls talking about men needing brides over in the Americas, in the west where the land was still unsettled and everyone worked hard together to make a new start.

She needed a new start.

So she'd secretly asked one of the servants to pick her up a copy of a newspaper she'd heard was advertising for brides. Until now, she'd been too afraid to even look, sure she'd never have the courage to head to a new country on her own.

But in her heart, she knew it was the answer she was searching for.

All she had to do was find someone who she believed would treat her well and who could accept her as she was.

As she started to read through the advertisements, she knew she'd found her chance for a fresh start of her own.

CHAPTER 2

"You're making wagers you better intend to pay on." Brooks Vaughn stared across the table at the man who had sweat dripping from his forehead as he looked down at the cards in his hand. The man swallowed, his throat moving up and down rapidly.

"Oh, I'm good for it. You just better make sure ye know what ye're doing."

Brooks almost laughed out loud at the shakiness of Milton Hayward's voice as he tried to bluff. He'd played enough hands of poker to know that Milton was about to lose.

Milton was a regular in the saloon they were sitting in and Brooks knew he likely didn't have the money to cover the wager he was laying down.

But Brooks didn't care.

He'd come here to make a name for himself and winning was what he needed to do.

Brooks had spent too many years playing the game, waiting for the chance to go up against another man, a man who'd cheated his father, eventually costing him his life. If he had to spend every day sitting in the saloons playing against lowlifes like Milton Hayward, he was willing to do just that.

All Brooks knew about the man who'd cheated his father was his given name—Virgil. He was a gambler who moved from town to town, cheating and winning from hard-working folk who were down on their luck, hoping for a better chance.

He also knew the man had a scar that stretched from the top of one eye, down his cheek to the corner of his lips. Brooks had heard it was from a run-in with another man who hadn't taken kindly to being cheated.

The other man had been killed but Virgil carried the scar that Brooks had spent years waiting to see sitting across the table from him.

Laying his cards on the table, he kept his eyes on Milton taking note of the exact moment the man realized he'd lost. Even though Brooks had spent years learning the craft of gambling and he still despised it, he had to admit to feeling a small rush of excitement every time he won.

He avoided playing against ordinary people who were hoping for a big win to help pay debts or feed their families. Taking money from men who weren't as practiced as he was would make him no better than the man who'd done the same to his father.

So Brooks only sought out the seedier characters to play against, the ones who spent their days cheating regular men from their hard-earned money.

Milton was one of those men. He could be found sitting at these tables any day or night of the week and he was well known to be a swindler who'd think nothing of placing wagers that would cost many men their entire livelihood.

But Milton was also not a smart player. Everything he won, he'd lose just as fast, unable to turn down another wager with other men who were better than him.

"Let's see your hand."

He waited for Milton to lay his cards on the table.

"There's no way ye coulda beat me," Milton hissed.

Brooks lifted an eyebrow and glared at the man. "Are you accusing me of cheating?" His voice was low but it carried a threat along with the question. Around here, if you were calling another man a cheater, you'd better have the proof to back it up.

Milton threw his cards on the table, scattering them among the money and other cards already lying down.

Brooks stood, ready for a confrontation just as Milton pushed his own chair back.

"I ain't accusin' ye of nothin'. But I'll be keepin' a closer eye on ye the next time I sit at a table with you. That's a promise."

The two of them stood glaring at each other, both with their hands placed on the edge of the table, daring the other to move.

"Is there a problem here, boys?" The sound of his friend's voice broke through Brooks' anger. He stood up straight and turned to face the town sheriff who'd just walked over.

"No problem at all, Lewis. Simply settling up the wager Milton here just lost. Isn't that right, Milton?" He turned back and smiled at the man who was still standing with his fists tightly at his sides, glaring at Brooks.

"That's right. No problems here, Sheriff." The words came out through clenched teeth.

"It's time to pay up, Milton. You made a fairly hefty bet on that last hand, so I hope you have the money to cover it." He was enjoying watching Milton scramble to come up with a way to pay his debt, the same way Milton had done to others.

Milton glanced at the sheriff who was still standing and watching the exchange, before bringing his eyes back to Brooks.

"I don't reckon I have the full amount at the moment. But I'm willin' to put somethin' else up until I can get the money to pay you." The man who'd always been willing to take anything he could get from others was now trying to find something he could use to pay Brooks.

Brooks loved watching him squirm.

"What if I'm not prepared to take your deal? What could you possibly have to offer that'd be worth what you're owing me?"

A sneer spread across Milton's face that made the hair on the back of Brooks' neck stand up. "Oh, I got something you'd like. I know you've got that sister of yers holed up out on your farm and it must be a worry when ye're in town playing cards."

Brooks strode over closer to Milton, uneasy with the direction he was going with his offer. "Leave my sister out of this." They lived alone and he was the only family she had left to help care for her.

Milton put his hands up in front of him as Brooks got near. "Whoa! I'm not suggestin' anything bad. In fact, what I've got to offer just might be something ye could use for her needs, as well as yer own."

The man wasn't making any sense at all.

"What are you offering, Milton? I don't have all day to stand here listening to you ramble."

Just then the door to the saloon opened and light spread into the room. Brooks shielded his eyes which had become accustomed to the darkness.

He could make out the silhouette of what

looked like a woman holding a bag. As his eyes adjusted, he saw her standing there in a long dress, with a bonnet covering her head. Her head scanned the crowd along the long bar, her eyes flickering away in obvious embarrassment at the imitation nude masterpieces of the Renaissance painters about the room. She looked respectable, not a shady woman or a saloon girl, and he had to admire her courage to walk into a seedy establishment like this on her own.

Milton gave a little laugh as he nodded his head in the direction of the door. "That's what I'm offerin'. A woman, just for you."

CHAPTER 3

F iona felt her stomach lurch as the smell from the dank room assaulted her nostrils. The foul stench of unwashed bodies, stale liquor, and a room that surely hadn't seen a washcloth in years created a smell unlike anything she'd encountered before.

After the weeks aboard a ship, stagecoach, and then a train, she was tired, hot, and ready to get some rest. The last thing she was prepared to deal with was a dingy saloon full of men who were all ogling her as she stood in the doorway.

Why had she ever agreed to this? What kind of man asked his future bride, who'd traveled thousands of miles on her own, to meet him at a saloon up the dust-laden street from the train depot?

She should have known right then what she was in for. But she hadn't wanted to admit to anyone she was having second thoughts.

After she'd announced she'd answered an advertisement to be a bride across the ocean in America, she couldn't back out, no matter how unsure she was about her decision.

When he'd sent the money for the ticket and added a note to head up the street to the Alamo Saloon on her arrival, saying she'd be sure to find him there—she'd almost changed her mind.

But she needed this second chance, and she was determined to make the best of whatever was in store for her. She'd convinced herself it was surely a common thing in the Americas to spend all of your time in a public house.

Now as she looked around, her heart sank to her toes. Any man she'd find hanging in this dank room in the middle of the afternoon wasn't anyone she wanted to know.

And definitely not someone she'd want to marry.

The entire room had gone quiet. It was obvious the patrons weren't used to a lady casually strolling through the doors.

"I'm looking for Mr. Milton Hayward." She tried to keep her voice from trembling as she put on a bravado she certainly wasn't feeling.

No one said anything until one man stepped forward and walked toward her. He was quite a bit shorter than her and surely didn't weigh much more than herself. His blond hair hung limply from his head, indicating it hadn't been washed in a long time.

"Well, you must be my blushing bride." As soon as he said the words, her stomach started to churn.

What had she done? Agreeing to marry a man she didn't know was quite simply the most foolish thing she'd ever done in her life. And now she was left here with no other options.

Milton put his hand out and took hers in his, lifting it to his lips to place a kiss on it. She was glad she was still wearing her gloves.

The smell of alcohol overtook her as he lifted his lips in what she assumed was an attempt at a smile. The corners went up but the smile didn't quite reach his eyes. In fact, his eyes were already moving up and down as he looked her over from head to toe.

Her other hand crossed instinctively over her chest.

Another man strode over and people moved out of his way as he passed. He was nicely dressed, with a black jacket over a vest. He looked out of place in the room but it was obvious he was well known here too.

Her heart skipped a beat as he got closer and his dark amber eyes met hers. His hair was black from what she could see poking out from beneath the hat he wore. Something about him scared her but she also sensed somehow that he wasn't a threat.

She still hadn't said anything, unsure how to handle the situation she found herself in.

Milton still held her hand and he tugged her forward toward the new man standing beside him.

"Brooks, I'd like ye to meet my new bride." Milton turned back to face her. "What'd you say yer name was again?"

She swallowed the lump that was forming in her throat from the unshed tears. They'd corresponded a few times over the past year and she'd shared everything about herself with the man she believed was to be her husband.

Including her name. Many times.

"My name is Miss Fiona Murphy." This time she couldn't keep the tremor from her voice as she looked into the dark eyes staring back at her. She was sure she could see pity in their depths as he put his hand out to take hers from Milton's.

"It's a pleasure to meet you, ma'am." He kept his eyes on hers as he lifted her hand to kiss the back as Milton had done. However, she didn't feel the same urge to yank her hand out of his grasp. "I'm Brooks Vaughn. If there's anything I can ever assist you with, just let me know."

She almost believed he was offering his help at this moment, sensing the horrible situation she'd found herself in.

"Funny thing you should mention it, Brooks. This filly here's what I was talking about. I'd be willin' to let ye hold on to her to help around the house with yer sister for a spell. I'll even let her help with any of yer own more 'personal' needs until the time I can come up with the money I'm owing you."

Fiona looked between the men. Milton grinned widely as he slapped Brooks on the back. Brooks hadn't even moved a muscle.

Slowly, his head turned toward Milton. "Am I hearing you right? You're offering a woman, whom I'm assuming you've lied to in order to get her to come out here and marry you, as payment for your wager?"

Fiona could feel the room start to spin. What was Brooks talking about? What wager?

Under the black stubble, the muscles in Brooks' cheek tightened as he clenched his teeth together.

"I didn't think even you could sink so low." His voice was quiet but it rumbled and echoed across the still silent room.

Her soon to be husband just shrugged. "Well, I don't got nothin' else to offer ye, so either ye take her or get nothing. The choice is yours." He turned back and let his gaze move up and down her body once more. "I'd reckon she'd be worth at least that amount."

Her entire body started to shake as she realized the man she'd come out here to marry was not the man he'd led her to believe in his letters. Additionally, he was now offering her as payment on a bet.

CHAPTER 4

B rooks swallowed hard as he fought to control his anger. He wasn't sure how Milton had convinced this woman to travel all this way to marry him but he was sure it wasn't by being honest.

And now he was prepared to settle his debt by offering her as payment until he had the money.

The worst part was, Brooks couldn't just leave her now to Milton, no matter how distasteful he found the agreement to be. He may be considered a scoundrel by many men but one thing he would never do is leave a woman in need to face someone like Milton Hayward on her own.

He found his eyes drawn to hers and her bright green eyes glistened from unshed tears. They were open wide and he could tell she was fighting hard not to let fear take over her.

"Where are you from?" He tried to keep his

voice low, hoping it would calm her a bit.

She lifted her chin and he watched her swallow hard. "I'm from London. I've been traveling for quite a while and, I must confess, I'm a bit confused and unsure exactly what's going on here."

He smiled as he realized she was no longer even acknowledging Milton, obviously believing he was the more trustworthy one.

"Well, Miss Murphy, it would appear you've been duped into agreeing to marry a snake who's lied to you. Whatever he told you in his correspondence to convince you to come all this way to marry him was a deception."

"That ain't true. And besides, ye don't know what I told 'er," Milton interrupted, pushing himself back between them.

Brooks let his gaze fall on the other man, resisting the urge to end the conversation with his fists. "I know enough to realize there's no way any woman would agree to marry you if she knew you."

Milton just snickered loudly. "She's the one who agreed to take my money for a ticket to come all this way without knowing me first. So, the way I see it, she's mine. Do you want to take her as payment until I can pay you the cash or not? This is yer last chance. Otherwise, I'll be taking 'er down the street to see the minister and then heading home to spend the night with my new bride."

Brooks cursed to himself silently as he saw the

terror flicker in the woman's eyes. She may have been naive in coming all this way on her own but she didn't deserve to be left with the likes of Milton Hayward.

"I'll agree to this only if you let go of any claim you have to her. We'll wipe your debt clean for your wager."

Milton gave a harsh laugh. "She owes me a great deal more than what I owed ye for our little bet. I paid a pretty penny to get this lass over here from England, so unless you plan to pay me for all that she owes me, I'll be taking her back after our debt is paid up."

Brooks had to hold himself back from grabbing Milton by the throat and dragging him outside. He could see he wasn't going to let go of his claim on this woman that easily.

He looked at Fiona who was standing perfectly still. The only thing that gave away her fear were her eyes. They flickered back and forth between the men and he knew she must be devastated at the situation unfolding in front of her.

"I'll take her."

The color drained from her face even more and he was sure she was going to faint.

Milton slapped him hard on the shoulder as he laughed loudly. "I knew ye couldn't refuse the offer of a woman for yer own use, even for a short time. I'll be in touch when I have the money for my wager." He winked at Brooks and the bile rose in his throat. "Ye take good care of my future wife."

Milton turned then and walked away without so much as a word of apology to the woman he'd lured out here across the ocean and the country.

Brooks was left standing with Miss Murphy and she still hadn't said a word as she watched the man walk away. When she finally turned back to face him, he recognized a spark of anger in the depths of her green eyes.

"Excuse me but I'm not a piece of property that can be pawned off between men. I'm not exactly sure what just happened here. I've spent weeks making my way to a strange country, on my own, under the impression I was coming out to meet an honorable man to marry. I won't just be passed off to some scoundrel who'd take a woman as payment for a debt." Her chin trembled, giving away the fear she was feeling beneath her anger.

He needed to get her out of this room where men were still sitting and watching the exchange.

Grabbing her elbow, he started to pull her toward the door. She resisted, pulling her arm from his grip. Sighing, he turned back around.

"Listen, Miss Murphy, I'm not happy with the arrangement either. But the way I see it, you don't have a whole lot of options at the moment. If you don't leave here with me, you'll be back in the hands of Milton Hayward within moments. He paid to bring you out here, so he believes you're rightfully his unless you can pay him the full amount back. Do you have access to that kind of money right now?"

He felt bad that he was having to shock her into listening but he wasn't in the mood to fight with a woman he hadn't even planned on having to deal with in the first place.

"I'm offering you the chance to walk out of here with me and I'll try to figure out how you can get yourself out of this mess. I may not be the best man you could end up with but I assure you, there are a lot more who'd have no trouble taking advantage of a woman on her own out here with no one to protect her. So, you can either stay here and take your chances on protecting yourself from Hayward and the other men who are already eyeing you up. Or you can let me get you out of here until we can figure out how to get you back home."

He watched her nervously twisting her hands in front of her where they were holding her one bag. Her steamer trunk was probably still at the station. Finally, she nodded her head.

"It seems I have no other choice." She lifted her chin and walked past him toward the doorway as though nothing out of the ordinary had just happened to her.

He was already regretting ever coming to this saloon today and he could see he was about to pay dearly for that decision.

CHAPTER 5

"I would say you're quite obviously in your cups if you think I'm getting up on that horse with you." Fiona had reached her breaking point.

She was tired, hungry, and had just been pawned off to a man to pay a debt. The last thing she was about to do was hop up onto a horse with that man who could take her to who knows where, and do who knows what to her.

Her innocence and desire to have a new life had gotten her into a real mess this time. Coming out here on her own was a huge mistake. She'd never even thought about all of the things that could happen to a woman on her own in a strange country.

But she was finding out quickly.

Now she was left standing in front of a saloon and no doubt, house of ill-repute, in a dusty town in

Kansas, arguing about how she was going to get back to a strange man's house.

She would laugh at the absurdity of it all if she wasn't so close to breaking down in tears.

The man in front of her pushed his hat back on his head and thrust his fingers through his hair in frustration. He sighed loudly as he set his hat back on his head.

"I'm about ready to leave you standing here on the street. I don't have the time to deal with any of this. I'm trying to help save you from a fate you quite obviously never considered when you answered an advertisement to come out here on your own. I'm tired. I'm hungry. And I'm sure you are too."

He placed one foot in the stirrup on the saddle and easily swung his leg up over the back of the horse. It was hard not to notice how large he appeared with the sun silhouetted behind him while he looked down at her.

"Now my sister is waiting at home for me and I'm sure she'd welcome the company. You can come with me on top of this horse or you can stand on the street and wait for the first man to accost you. And I assure you, the dust won't even have settled around your feet before that happens. I'm leaving now, so the choice is yours."

He reached his hand down and the darkness was apparent in his eyes as he stared at her.

What choice did she have?

She put her hand in his, and before she even had a chance to prepare, she was being lifted up from the ground. She let out a high-pitched screech as he plopped her sideways onto his lap.

Without thinking, she reached up to make sure her bonnet was pulled down and her collar pulled up on the side facing him. She didn't know why she cared what he thought but it was a habit that she always tried to cover it up.

"Sit still and hold on to your bag or you'll be lying on the ground under Buck's hooves. We can arrange for your steamer truck to come out in a wagon later."

He hadn't even finished his sentence, never mind given her a chance to grab her carpet bag, before he'd kicked his heels into the horse's sides and they were off.

She didn't know what to hang on to as they flew down the street at a breakneck speed, so she just grabbed for the first thing she could.

The fact that it was his arm didn't matter to her. She knew if she didn't hang on, she'd be left behind sitting among her skirts in the dust.

Her body fell flat against his chest, and she was almost sure she could feel his chest rumble with laughter as they rode away. If she survived the ride to his farm in one piece, she planned to let him know exactly how much she did not appreciate this reckless ride.

Her cheeks burned as she realized how close she was to him. She felt the strength in his chest and, strangely, she felt a sense of security in his arms. Somehow, she knew he was the only thing preventing her from certain death under the horse's pounding hooves.

With the jarring of the horse, she was having a difficult time focusing on the landscape around her which was so different from home. But as they raced around a corner and came into a clearing, a little house sat amid some trees.

Brooks finally slowed down, seeming to find a calmness as he came closer to the home. She could make out a creek running behind the house and there appeared to be a garden off to the side.

She tried to pull herself up to a more appropriate distance from him as they slowed but she began to slip sideways as she moved.

"Just sit tight. We're almost home." His voice was deep in her ear and sent a shiver down her spine at the huskiness of the sound. His arms tightened around her waist and her pulse quickened.

What she wouldn't give for a good night's rest at the moment. She was sure her senses were completely rattled.

They pulled up in front of the house and as she tried to adjust her skirts and rearrange herself, he jumped down from the horse without giving her any warning to grab on to the saddle.

Before she could stop it, she started to topple backward, frantically trying to grasp something to stop her fall. But before she hit the ground, she landed unceremoniously into the strong arms of the man who'd made her fall in the first place.

He was grinning down at her and his eyes held a hint of sparkle in their amber depths. "I must say, this is the fastest I've ever had a woman I just met fall into my arms."

She tried to push herself up but he wasn't letting go.

"Put me down, you heathen," her words hissed out between clenched teeth. He may be used to having women swoon at his feet but she wasn't about to be one of those women.

"Brooks, let the poor woman go." A woman's voice came up behind her, softly chastising the man who was holding her.

"Oh, Lydia, you're spoiling all my fun." He let her legs go, keeping his other arm behind her back as he still held her close. His eyes never left hers and as her entire body heated with embarrassment, he winked at her.

Finally getting her senses under control, she pushed herself away from him and busied herself with brushing the wrinkles out of her skirt as she tried to slow her breathing down.

He reached down to pick up her bag that had landed in a heap on the ground as she fell. "Lydia, this is Miss Fiona Murphy. She came out west to marry Milton Hayward but due to some unforeseen circumstances, and luckily for her, I ended up with her instead."

"What? What are you talking about, Brooks?"

Lydia came over and reached out to take Fiona's hands in hers. Fiona was, finally, able to look up and for the first time since she'd arrived, she found herself looking into kind eyes that were focused on her with genuine concern.

Unable to stop herself, tears started falling down her cheeks. Seeming to understand, the woman dropped her hands and pulled her into her arms.

"Brooks Vaughn! What have you done to this poor girl?"

CHAPTER 6

Brooks walked out of the barn, throwing the bucket he held off to the side. His mood had turned even more foul after they'd arrived back home. He'd dealt with Milton and thought he was doing the right thing by trying to save Fiona from a fate worse than death. But he'd been scolded like a child by his younger sister as though he'd done something wrong.

He admitted perhaps he'd been a bit insensitive to the woman. But the truth was, he'd been fed up with the whole situation and really didn't have any patience left by the time he'd dragged her onto his horse.

Then when her body had fallen into his chest, a strange feeling of protection had washed over him and he hadn't been sure what to make of it.

He'd hoped his teasing would lighten the mood,

instead it'd brought the poor woman to tears. He'd soon found out she wasn't like most women who threw themselves easily at his feet with just a simple wink.

As he came through the door to the house, the two women sat side by side at the table with a cup of tea. The smell of roast chicken filled the room and set his stomach grumbling.

"Everyone all right?" he asked the question of his sister but kept his eyes on Fiona sitting with her head down, staring at the cup in her hand.

Lydia reached her hand out to squeeze Fiona's hand as she smiled at her. "I think so. Nothing a good night's rest and some decent food in her stomach won't fix."

He nodded, then moved over to the basin to wash his hands.

"I should offer you my thanks, Mr. Vaughn, for bringing me here. I hope you'll understand my concerns and worry back in town. I'd been traveling for many weeks, then just found out everything I'd been coming here for had been a lie. My chance at a new life had been ripped from my grasp before I was even able to wipe the dust from my travel-worn dress."

He turned, taking the towel to dry his hands as he leaned back against the cabinet. Fiona had lifted her head and, for the first time, he was able to get a good look at her.

He'd noticed how green her eyes were but not how bright they shone against the white of her skin. Her hair was a deep red, with streaks of every other shade of red woven through it. It hung in a single length of thick ringlets over her shoulder against her bosom. Loose curls framed her face, with no doubt, a swept up, elaborately styled, London high bun pinned up under the bonnet.

He found himself at a loss for words as he stared. He couldn't seem to tear his eyes away from her. And as he watched, she once again reached up and pulled the collar of her dress up.

Before she could cover it up, though, he noticed the red mark that trailed down from her jaw and under the fabric.

He made himself tear his gaze away, knowing by the shade of red making its way up her cheeks that he was making her uncomfortable. He simply nodded in her direction, not trusting himself to speak yet.

He pushed himself away from the cabinet and walked over to the table. "I've invited Miss Murphy to stay here as long as she needs to until she can get back home."

"It'll be nice to have the company," said Lydia, clearing the tea things and setting the table for a meal.

"May I help you?" said Fiona.

"No, sit a while and rest." Lydia set the food on the table as Brooks sat down across from Fiona.

"Well, we still have the problem of paying Milton back for her ticket out here. I can't imagine he'll just let that go. As long as he still owes me for our wager today, she's safe here. But as soon as he gets the money to pay up, he'll be coming for her." He picked up a chicken leg and set it on his plate.

"Brooks! Could you please be a little more sensitive?" He lifted his eyes at his sister's shocked voice and looked at Fiona.

She sat looking at him with her eyes unblinking across the table.

"That's all right, Lydia. He's only speaking the truth. Now that I've had some time to think about it, I realize I need to find a way out of this mess. I should have let my sister come with me when she offered so, at least, I wouldn't have been alone out here. Although I doubt there's much she could have done to help."

She took a bite of the chicken that had been set in front of her and he watched as her eyes closed and she savored every bite. They ate in silence and he smiled to himself as she delicately cut her food with her knife and fork. She pushed the food onto the fork tines with her knife in the English way, not scooping it up like he was used to seeing. Each forkful into her mouth was as though she'd been starving. As he looked at her, he realized she very likely was.

Coming over on the ship and then making her way west had to have been hard on her own. Most women would have a hard time doing that, yet he hadn't heard her complain about it once.

This was most likely her first full and hot meal since she'd left London weeks ago. And she was a small slip of a girl who really couldn't afford to miss many meals by the looks of her.

When she was finished, she set her knife and fork down, and dabbed at her mouth lightly with the napkin in her lap. "Excuse my rudeness. I guess I didn't realize quite how hungry I was." Her cheeks had gone a bright shade of red again.

His sister patted her arm before taking another helping of the chicken and placing it on Fiona's plate. "Don't be embarrassed. After everything you've been through, I have no doubt you're famished."

Fiona's eyes met his across the table as he watched her table manners, indicating she wasn't a lowly peasant girl in any way where she came from.

"So, where did you say you were from exactly? And why did you feel the need to come all this way to marry a stranger, when it's quite apparent you have been raised with money and status?"

He sat back in his chair and crossed his arms across his chest. Something didn't seem right about her story. A woman who'd, obviously, had a good upbringing in a wealthy family shouldn't need to be coming out here to marry a man like Milton Hayward.

She lifted her chin and placed her napkin neatly to the side of her plate. Her eyes met his and he was sure he saw them flash an even brighter shade of green.

"I was raised in the country outside of London until my mother passed away a few years ago and my father remarried. He married a widow from an upper-class family and she insisted we all be trained in proper manners and etiquette. Something, I must say, I've seen sorely lacking by many people since I've arrived here." He was sure her chin rose a notch higher as he aimed her words at him.

"And my reasons for coming here are my own and of no concern to you. While I appreciate you coming to my aid, it doesn't give you the right to be privy to all details of my life."

She turned to look at Lydia who had a grin that covered her entire face. "If you don't mind, Lydia, I'll take my leave and turn in. I am exhausted." She never even gave him another glance.

He stood as she did and watched as she tugged at the collar of her dress again, making sure it covered as much of the mark on her neck as possible. He was sure she didn't even notice she did it. It was a habit but he didn't know why she bothered—it didn't take anything away from her beauty.

"Please, don't get up. Good night everyone."

He sat back down with his sister at the table, watching until she'd gone into the room she and Lydia would share. When the door shut, Lydia turned to him with her face still grinning.

"Looks like you've finally met a woman who isn't afraid to put you in your place and who won't fall swooning at your feet with the slightest show of your dimples, Brooks Vaughn."

He scowled back at her, then stood to go back out and finish the chores. He didn't care what she said. There had to be some reason she came all the way here and he intended to find out what it was.

CHAPTER 7

"So, if you don't mind me asking, where exactly does Brooks go every day?" Fiona lifted her hand to shield her eyes from the sun as she crouched down beside the creek with the wicker basket full of clothes.

Lydia struggled to sit on a rock, limping to the side and using her hands to help ease herself down. Fiona had never asked her about her ailment, believing her new friend would tell her when she was ready.

She'd been here for a few days already and, each day, Brooks would head into Abilene and they wouldn't see him until the end of the day. She wasn't certain if it was just her but surely he was growing more cantankerous every time she saw him.

But she'd built a wonderful friendship with

Lydia and was so grateful to have her. She sensed that the other woman welcomed the company too.

Lydia bent down into the water and dunked the shirt she was holding before pulling it out to rub it on the washboard they'd carried down. She was certainly learning new skills, one would never have thought she'd ever have to employ.

"Brooks has an insatiable thirst for revenge against a man who he feels wronged our father and, ultimately, caused the death of our parents. He can't see past the anger he's carried all these years to realize he's wasting his life waiting for the opportunity to make the man pay."

Fiona wrung out the blouse she was washing. She'd seen a few items that belonged to Brooks in the basket but she'd gone out of her way to avoid having to handle any of his clothing, choosing one of Lydia's skirts instead.

Lydia looked out past the creek into the distance. "Our pa worked hard and had a dream of making this farm into something special. Life was good and we had a happy family. Then one summer, when I was still young and stubborn, I insisted I could ride our horse without any help. I'd been told so many times that I still needed someone to lead me until I was ready but I wouldn't listen. Brooks was the only one who believed me and he helped me up onto the horse against our parents' wishes when they were busy out in the field."

She hesitated for a moment. "When I fell from the horse, I almost died."

There was a tremor in Lydia's voice as she quietly said the words. Fiona stood and moved over to sit beside her friend on the rock.

"I was in bed for a long time and it took a lot of doctor's visits after that to try and fix my leg. It didn't set properly but my father insisted we had to find the best doctors. It cost a lot of money we didn't have." Lydia looked down at the shirt she was still holding in her hands.

"One day in town, after taking the final bit of the year's crops in to pay off some of the bills, he met a man who sweet talked him into a game of cards. He told him if he won, he'd have all the money he'd need to pay his bills and plenty left over to find the best doctors out there."

Fiona sensed Lydia's need to tell her story even though it was painful. Putting her arm across her shoulders, she remained silent and let her continue.

"He lost all his money. He couldn't even pay the bills he had in town and he knew then we'd never be able to afford a doctor who could help me. Shortly after that, my ma came down with pneumonia and died. Pa just couldn't take any more. Brooks went out one morning to do chores and he found pa's body in the barn. He never told me what happened or what he found but it's eaten him alive every day since."

Lydia looked at her with eyes wet with tears. "He's always blamed himself. He put me on the horse that day. After our parents were gone, he took it on his shoulders to look after me and the farm pa had worked so hard to build. But he also decided he'd make the man who'd taken advantage of our pa pay for what he did."

"Does the man live here? Surely he knew what your family was going through. How could he have taken money from your father like that?"

Lydia laughed sadly. "It's not like London where people are maybe a bit more civilized, I'm afraid. Out here, there are so many swindlers and cheaters who don't care about anyone but themselves. You're at their mercy if you don't learn how to beat them at their own game. And that's exactly what Brooks has spent the past few years doing. The man who beat our pa doesn't live around here and he's only been back around a few times since. He travels from town to town, cheating hard-working folks from their money."

"So Brooks is ensuring he becomes good enough to sit at a table with him and beat him at his game..." Fiona finished, finally understanding why Brooks headed to town every day to gamble.

"I've tried to tell him to just let it go. It's time to move on and let what happened in the past stay there but he can't. He gets up at the crack of dawn every day to work the farm, then cleans up and heads to town to hang with all of the lowlifes who spend their days in the saloons. He never plays anyone who can't afford it or who he'd be taking advantage of. And, he makes sure no one else does it while he's around to stop it." Lydia gave a slight shrug as she wrung out the shirt in her hands.

"Then, he comes home and spends the rest of the day working his fingers to the bone to provide for me and to care for this farm. It's all we have left of our parents and he's determined we'll never lose it."

Fiona let her eyes scan the fields around her and the land she was sitting on. It was beautiful here and she could understand why Brooks never wanted to lose it.

"I'm not much help around the farm. I can do some of the duties like laundry and cooking for him and I tend the garden but I'm afraid my leg doesn't allow me to do much else."

Fiona's heart ached for the woman beside her. And if she was being honest with herself, for the man who obviously carried the weight of guilt that wasn't his to carry.

She suddenly realized that her own problems, and her own insecurities about a small mark on her neck, were trivial in comparison to what this family had endured.

Somehow, she knew she had to help them heal.

CHAPTER 8

"I'm still not convinced this is a good idea. I don't know why you ladies can't listen to common sense." Brooks was irritated and he didn't care if they knew it. The last thing he had time for was driving two women into town, then keeping an eye on them when the leeches and snakes started to find them.

Abilene wasn't any place for a lady. As a hustling cow town, the people who usually found themselves on the streets weren't the kind of people you'd want to get to know any better.

But they'd insisted he take them or they'd go themselves. He wasn't sure Fiona was a very good influence on his sister, who'd never threatened to head in to town on her own before. She'd always been content to stay on the farm and away from the stares of the townsfolk.

"Mr. Vaughn, I need to get a wire to my father. He can telegraph some money to me so I can pay Milton what he's owed, so I can return home. I wish there was some other way than having to ask for help from my father but I don't know what else to do. He was never happy about me coming out here to begin with and it's humiliating enough to have to go begging to him now for assistance."

Her skin had more color than when she'd first arrived just over a week ago and he noticed she'd let her hair go a little looser too. She'd adjusted well to life out here, which surprised him.

When he'd first seen her, he thought she'd never survive away from the comforts she was quite obviously used to in London.

But she'd been helping Lydia around the house and spending a great deal of time outdoors helping in the garden too. He was glad to see Lydia smile so much, having a friend to spend time with after years of being alone on the farm.

He hated that she had to stay out there on her own but he never wanted her around the despicable people who wandered the streets of Abilene. The few times she'd accompanied him to town, he knew she'd suffered the humiliation as people stared at her awkward gait as she walked down the street.

"Well, we'll stop at the wire office and you can send your message. But we won't be hanging around." He leaned forward to look past his sister to

Fiona sitting on the outside of the bench in the wagon. "You realize we could very likely run into your charming husband-to-be?"

He had no doubt Milton would be hanging around town. He was there every day, swindling and drinking, and Brooks knew they'd be in for a confrontation from the man.

But he seemed to be the only one who cared.

"I realize that. And he's not my husband-to-be. When my father wires my money, I will pay Milton and this will all be over."

Brooks had to laugh. "Do you seriously think Hayward will just back down like that? Even if you pay him back, I assure you, he won't let you go that easily. In case you hadn't noticed, there aren't a whole lot of options for men out here as far as women go. And even less for men like him."

"Well then, we'll just have to go to the law and let them know what he's up to if he does decide to make a fuss."

He almost dropped the reins from his hands. *Make a fuss?* That's what she thought he'd do?

She really was far from the London society she was used to.

Yanking on the reins as the buildings of Abilene appeared in the distance, he stopped the wagon and turned in his seat to make sure she had to look at him.

"I don't think you have any idea just what a man

like Hayward can do if he doesn't get his way. He'll do much more than 'make a fuss,' I assure you of that. And I think it's best if you prepare yourself for that. I still don't know how I can hold him off once he has the money to pay the debt he owes me. You're just lucky I'm a betting man and was willing to gamble that day. Or you'd be unhappily married to Hayward with no one to help you."

"Brooks. Stop being so harsh. She doesn't need to be reminded about any of that. The fact is, for now, she's safe with us. And I know you aren't the type of man who'd let someone like Mr. Hayward hurt a woman, no matter how tough you try to act. You'd never have let him take her home even if you hadn't won that bet."

Lydia slapped him on the arm as she turned to face Fiona. "Don't listen to him. He's just overprotective and he seems to think everyone would just be safer left out on a farm, away from the debauchery present in town."

He shook his head at his sister's choice of words. She wondered why he worried about her.

The two women beside him didn't seem to realize it was going to be him who'd have to protect them in town, so he had every right to be harsh. He had a reputation around town as a man not to be messed with but he knew two proper women walking around town would be too tempting for most men to ignore.

44

Flicking the reins, he let the horses lead them into town. The sooner he got this over with, the sooner he could be back home to drop the women off. He'd been hearing rumors that Virgil was back in the area and he knew he'd make his way here.

Babysitting two women wasn't in his plans. He wanted to make sure he was in town when the man showed up. And this time, he was going to make him sit across the table from him.

It was time to make him pay.

CHAPTER 9

"So, any idea how you're going to get Fiona back home and away from Milton?" Lewis Kinkaid was just one of the acting sheriffs in Abilene, at the moment. There were usually a few on the payroll and because it was such a dangerous and thankless job, there was a high turnover rate.

Lewis had been in town for close to three years already, so he was considered to be a senior member. He and Brooks had become close friends in that time. Even though Brooks was considered to be a bit of a ruffian and a rake by the people in town, Lewis was one of the few people who knew why Brooks was spending so much time in the saloons.

Brooks had helped Lewis a few times with the arrests of people who weren't cooperating and they'd built a level of trust between the two of them.

Now, as he stood with his booted foot resting up on the side of his wagon in front of the sheriff's office, Brooks found he didn't want to talk about the woman in question.

"I have no idea and I'm still not sure how I ever let myself get dragged into this mess in the first place. I've got more important things to be worrying about."

"Oh, yes. I'd heard Virgil was back in the area. I'm sure we'll know soon enough when he shows up in town." Lewis looked across the street to where the two women were now coming out of the wire office.

Brooks noticed his friend's eyes on his sister and he instantly felt a need to protect her from his stare. Before he could say anything though, Lewis interrupted.

"Your sister's quite a looker, Brooks. I can see she got all the looks in your family."

Brooks found himself relaxing a bit as he realized his friend was looking at the woman past her limp.

"Yes, she is. And that's why I make sure she doesn't come to town where she can be taken advantage of by any of the scum who wander the streets here."

Brooks ignored the look his friend sent his way.

"It must be nice for her to have some company."

He just nodded, not wanting to talk about his sister anymore either.

But Lewis, obviously, didn't realize his friend wasn't in a talking mood. "Well, at any rate, you better figure something out for Miss Murphy. I'm not sure Milton's going to let her go that easily. Even if she does get the money to pay him back."

Brooks leaned back and looked at Lewis. "You're the sheriff. Surely, there's something you can do to help her. Why is this suddenly my problem?" Brooks was aggravated. He was still wishing he'd never gone to the saloon that day. Now, he was stuck trying to sort out a problem that shouldn't be his to deal with.

"I've looked into what I can do. My hands are tied as long as she owes him the money. I can try to keep him from forcing her to go with him but I can't promise much more than that. Unfortunately, around these parts, sometimes what's right and wrong don't matter much. I do my best to keep things under control but even I can't be with her and protecting her every hour of the day." Lewis leaned his foot up next to his.

"And besides, it's Milton Hayward we're talking about. He does things his own way and doesn't pay any mind to the law."

They both stood in silence watching the women now go into the mercantile. Brooks heard himself sigh. He'd told them to hurry and now they were going in to do some shopping.

As he shook his head, he noticed the man who'd also spotted the women heading into the store.

Swearing loudly, he pushed himself away from the wagon and strode across the street as though the devil was on his heels. But he knew the devil was actually making his way toward the women inside the store.

He heard Lewis curse as he followed behind him.

"Get your hands off me, you filthy man. I'd rather be dragged behind a galloping horse through a patch of wild cactus than ever go anywhere with the likes of you."

The sound of Fiona's enraged voice filled his ears the moment he came through the door. If not for the seriousness of the situation, he'd have laughed out loud at the look he saw on Milton's face as she let him know exactly what she thought of him.

But the shock didn't last long and fury took over Milton's face.

"Well, yer opinion of me don't make a lick of difference one way or another. I've got the money to pay Brooks back, so now that he's had his fun with ye, it's my turn." Milton sneered in her face and Brooks had to stop himself from slamming his fist into Milton's nose.

His stomach sunk, though, as he realized what

Milton had said. If he had the money, he was going to have to figure out a way to buy them some more time.

And no matter how much he tried to figure it out, he wasn't even sure why he felt it was up to him to save this woman anyway.

"Milton. Take your hands off her." His voice left no doubt that he wasn't in the mood to argue.

The other man let his hands drop but he laughed with a wicked sound that set the hair on the back of his neck on end.

"Ye seem to forget that she's mine. I only let ye borrow her for a spell." As Brooks looked at Milton, he realized that the man seriously believed he was on the same level as him. And that they were kindred spirits who shared a love for gambling and having some fun with this woman.

Brooks felt like knocking the man to the ground. Maybe he could use that realization to his advantage.

"I'll play you for her. For one more week." The man's laugh made his stomach churn.

"So, ye ain't finished with her yet. I knew you'd like havin' yer own woman around to help fill yer needs for a while."

Brooks caught Fiona's shocked stare. He put his most rakish grin on his face. "Well, you were certainly right about that, Milton."

Milton laughed again and slapped him hard on the back. Brooks had to fight the urge to cringe.

He kept his eyes on Fiona and he watched her shocked expression turn to one of seething rage as she realized he was about to place a bet and gamble on her. He could tell she wasn't too happy about the fact or the insinuation he'd made about what'd happened between the two of them while she'd been staying with him.

"Ye know I can't resist a good wager. So, what'll you put up in return? What'll ye pay me if I win?" Brooks knew that'd never happen.

"My farm."

He ignored the shocked outburst he heard all around him as he watched the other man. That was a bet he knew he couldn't turn down.

"You've got yerself a wager."

CHAPTER 10

Fiona's heart was beating so hard she was sure they could see the fabric moving on her dress. She wasn't sure if it was from fear or anger but she suspected it was surely some of both.

How could Brooks have made a wager on her? And then to put his farm on the line as the wager?

She was livid.

As they'd made their way to the dark saloon, where she and Lydia were made to stand outside, she'd pleaded with Sheriff Kinkaid to do something, insisting that surely there was something he could do.

He'd said that out here, sometimes the law didn't matter. She owed Milton a debt that until she paid up he didn't have many options to help her.

Then he'd insisted she'd be fine. He said Brooks

wouldn't let anything happen to her and that she was lucky to have him on her side.

At the moment, she'd rather be on a ship back to England where men were a bit more civilized. She was sure men over there would never gamble on a woman as she was being forced to endure.

But no matter how angry she was, she was also feeling a twinge of worry that Brooks might not win. Even though she was furious with him at the moment for making this wager, she also knew if he hadn't, she'd surely be on her way home with Milton.

She shivered as she thought about it.

"Don't worry, Fiona. I'm sure Brooks knows what he's doing." Lydia leaned in close and whispered in her ear, "He'd never put the farm up if he didn't think he'd win."

She didn't know what to say to her friend. "I'm quite fed up with all of this, to be honest. I can't believe I'm standing here waiting to see who'll win me. I don't know whether I should laugh at the absurdity of it or fall to the ground in a crying heap."

As she watched from the open doorway, the dust from the street swirled around her legs, and Milton and Brooks stared hard at each other across the table. Neither of them were ready to back down.

"Lay them out, Hayward. Time to see who won."

Fiona felt her mouth go dry. What if Brooks

didn't win? Surely someone would help her, and stop Milton from taking her. They wouldn't all just sit back and let him win, would they?

She tried to act like she didn't care, and that she was too angry to be worried. But in truth, she was terrified. She knew what a horrible mistake it'd been to come here, believing the man she'd been writing to was honest and good. And now she was relying on a stranger to continue helping her when he'd already done more than he needed to.

Lifting her chin, she put on a brave face, determined that if Milton won, she'd run from here and find somewhere to hide.

Brooks caught her eye from where he sat at the table just inside the door and her heart lurched as he winked at her. Somehow, sensing his sureness put her at ease. She could tell he was used to having women fall at his feet with a subtle wink and if she wasn't so afraid at the moment, she was ashamed to admit, it might've worked on her too.

"Sorry, Hayward. Looks like I've won myself the lovely lady for one more week."

Milton was sputtering and swearing. "Don't know how you keep beating me but ye can be sure, after this week, I'm taking what's rightfully mine." He stood up quickly, knocking over a chair behind him and scowled at her as he walked past.

"Enjoy yer time with Brooks, because once he's done with ye, ye're all mine."

Her body started to tremble as she watched him swagger away. She only had one more week to find a way out of this mess. If the money didn't get here soon, she didn't know what she'd do.

Before she had time to think about it any longer, Brooks had his hand on her elbow and was practically dragging her from the wooden sidewalk in front of the saloon.

Lydia followed behind as quickly as she could.

Finding herself out in the bright sunlight once again, she had to squint until her eyes adjusted. She pulled hard on her arm.

"Mr. Vaughn, I'm quite capable of walking across the street to the wagon. I don't need you dragging me like a sack of potatoes."

He stopped and tilted his head to the side. "I'm quite sure you can. However, since you're the one who insisted on coming into town in the first place, then insisted on going to the mercantile, after I'd specifically told you to hurry and not make any extra stops, I think I'm quite deserving to drag you back to the wagon however I see fit."

She clenched her fists at her side as she glared at him. "I had to come to town to send a wire to my father. And just because I chose to stop at the mercantile doesn't give that man the right to accost me. Or give you the right to make a bet on me. What if you'd lost, Mr. Vaughn? Did you ever think of that?"

She knew she should be thanking him for everything he'd done for her but, for some reason, she was irked and she had to let him know.

He laughed. "Of course I thought about that. It was a chance I was willing to take." He was grinning at her with that rakish smile she vowed would never work on her.

Lifting her chin in the air, she walked past him onto the street without giving him another glance.

Before she could get any farther, hands were on her waist, and her feet lifted from the ground.

"And another thing. I wouldn't drag a sack of potatoes. I'd be sure to fling it over my shoulder for easier carrying." His voice laughed up at her as she pounded on his back, yelling to let her go.

She thought she'd been angry before but that was nothing until she was carried down the street over his shoulder to the waiting wagon.

She almost believed Milton Hayward might have been the better option.

CHAPTER 11

The sun beat down on his back, and the sweat dripped into his eyes from the hair that was poking out beneath the hat. He'd spent the day in the field, choosing not to go into town today.

After yesterday, he wanted to let Hayward have a day to cool down before seeing him again.

Not to mention he had a crop to get off the field, and time was running out to finish. Even though he made money from his gambling, all of the winnings went into his farm. Times had been tough the past few years and while he always kept enough out to play another hand at the tables, he had to use some of the winnings to keep things going.

It was hard for him to be working on his own in the fields but he couldn't ask Lydia to help. She worked hard to keep the house and to make sure he was fed.

Some days, though, he wished he had family or someone else around who could lend a hand.

He had the few acres of land he planted wheat on but he also had to tend to the cattle. It wasn't a big herd by any means but he'd managed to buy a few head and was determined he'd make a living from his farm.

Stopping to lean against the scythe he held in his hands, he stretched and looked toward the house. His hand went up to shield his eyes as someone walked in his direction.

Fiona was picking her way across the field wearing a skirt and blouse she'd obviously borrowed from his sister. Instead of the regular, brightly colored silks she usually wore, he found himself catching his breath as he noticed how stunning she looked in the light brown of the sturdier fabric she was wearing.

She looked like she'd grown up out here, washing clothes in the creek and planting gardens in the dirt, instead of sitting in the London ballrooms.

"Can I help you with something, Miss Murphy?" She hadn't spoken more than a few words to him since yesterday when they'd been in town. He couldn't figure out what she'd be doing coming out here.

Reaching her hand out to him, she offered him a cup filled with cold water from the metal pail she'd carried out with her. "I thought maybe you could use a hand."

His eyebrow moved up on its own. "You want to help me out here in the field? In this sweltering heat?" He tipped his head back and let the cool liquid coat his dry throat. He briefly worried that she might have thrown some poison into the water but decided he was too thirsty to care.

He held his smile back as he watched her clench her teeth together.

"Well, you've done so much to help me since I arrived in town and I'd like to do something to earn my keep. To try and pay you back in some way."

"Saving damsels in distress is just what I do. No need to repay me." He had to admit to himself, he admired her coming out to even offer her help. Most women would be content to let a man rescue her without feeling obligated to repay them somehow.

He tipped his head to one side. "Besides, I'd started to get the feeling maybe you weren't talking to me anymore." He didn't know why he felt the urge to get her riled up, knowing the mention of what happened yesterday, and the resulting hours of ignoring him would make her angry.

Her eyes flashed, and he shook his head as she squinted her eyes together. He'd known exactly how she'd react.

"Well, being thrown over your shoulder in town

wasn't the proper thing to do at all. What must everyone who witnessed that think? It was humiliating and uncalled for." Her arms crossed in front of her.

"You're right."

"And furthermore, gambling on a woman is a most uncouth..." She stopped as she finally heard the words he'd said. "I beg your pardon?"

He let his smile cover his face, knowing how it disarmed most women. "I said, you're right. It wasn't the proper thing to do at all." He leaned a little closer to her. "But one thing you'll learn about me, Miss Murphy, is that I'm not usually a man who does things that are proper."

He started swinging the blade again, knocking the wheat down in his path. He didn't have time for idle chitchat.

"You may as well find me something to do, or I'll just follow you along through the field and annoy you."

He lifted his head. She was still standing there with her hands neatly held in front.

"You think you can handle swinging this blade? Your arms don't look like they've got the strength to lift more than a hairbrush to fix your perfectly kept hair. I'm sure in London you didn't have to do much more than sit around and wait for your next suitor to come calling."

"You're always making comments about my

pampered life in London. Did you ever think to ask me about my life before we moved to London? Before my mother died? No, you haven't. And, I would wager you have no idea just how much I can do if I have to. I didn't lead the sheltered and pampered life you think I did. I wasn't doted on by servants my whole life and I didn't have suitors coming to call. I wasn't what you'd consider a *desirable* catch."

Her voice choked on the last words but she kept her eyes on him, and he watched as she crossed her arms over her chest.

Holding the scythe in front of him, he found his eyes squinting as he looked at her.

"I'm supposed to believe you didn't have a line-up of suitors at your door?" He couldn't believe it. The men in England must either be all blind or a bunch of witless dandy's who couldn't see what was right in front of their faces.

The color rose in her cheeks and he watched her reach up and pull at the collar of her blouse. She swallowed hard as she lifted her chin a bit higher.

She wouldn't say anything else and he felt his heart give a little tug as he realized she was serious. And from the way she always tried to cover the mark on her jaw, he had a pretty good idea why.

"Well, the men from your London society are a bunch of spineless fools."

Her eyes widened and he could sense her disbelief as she stood, unsure what to say.

"I always thought so." She gave him a weak smile.

The sadness he could see in her eyes finally explained to him why she'd come out west in the first place. He shook his head as he fought against a sudden anger that overwhelmed him.

She'd never felt good enough in London and the west held hopes of something better. Hoping someone could see her beauty.

Instead, she'd walked right into the arms of Milton Hayward.

He didn't know how he was going to do it but he knew then he wasn't about to ever let Milton get his hands on her. She'd been through enough already.

CHAPTER 12

Fighting back the tears, she turned to walk back outside. Brooks stood by the wagon where he'd parked directly in front of the wire office this time. He'd said he wasn't going to give her any chance of wandering off and getting herself in trouble again.

The past week with Lydia had been wonderful. She found herself being able to relax, something she hadn't done in years. She enjoyed working in the garden with her and she was learning how to make preserves from the vegetables they were gathering. It was a long way from the London society she'd lived in the past few years but it made her feel happier than she could ever remember.

Brooks had been around a bit, between working the field and going to town. After the day she'd gone to help him in the field, he hadn't seemed as grumpy to be around. He let her help him do some of the chores and they actually seemed to be getting along nicely.

But she knew he was going to be angry now when she came out. Tomorrow was the last day of the week she'd been given by Milton to get the money. It wasn't here yet and she hadn't even heard from her father.

Her mind raced as she tried to think of a way out of this mess. She'd already decided she would run if she had to and Lydia had some money saved up that she'd offered to give her.

Fiona knew it wouldn't get her far, though, and then she'd be left at the mercy of strangers again. At least here, she knew she had at least a few people who could try to help her.

Brooks was watching the door. Even from where she was standing, he must be well aware of her wringing her hands together. His eyes were already glaring.

He knew she didn't have the money.

Taking a deep breath, she opened the door and walked outside. She hoped the fear gripping her didn't show in her face.

"Nothing yet. I'm sure, by tomorrow, he'll have replied." She wished she could believe that but something told her her stepmother was making sure she was taught a lesson. They hadn't been happy about her coming out here on her own for different reasons of course.

Her father was worried for her but her step-mother didn't like how it looked for the family. She was sure they'd be the talk of society for weeks, having a daughter run off to America in the middle of the season.

Brooks didn't say a word but the muscles twitched in his jaw.

She swallowed slowly, hoping the movement would help calm her racing heart. She looked up to Lydia sitting on the wagon seat and tried not to let the tears fall that threatened when she saw the worry in her friend's eyes.

"Get in the wagon." Brooks was beside her, grabbing her elbow and pushing her toward it before she'd even realized he'd moved. "We need to get you out of town before Milton sees you. Doesn't matter that we still have a day to our agreement. If he sees you, he isn't going to wait anymore."

Just as she turned to take his hand to let him help her up into the wagon, the hair on her neck tingled at the sound of the voice behind her.

They were too late.

"Awful nice of ye to bring'er back a day early for me, Vaughn. I've been a patient man but not anymore. She's going to get her chance to be a blushing bride today."

She hadn't turned around and still stood with

one foot on the step up to the wagon. Brooks held her arm and she felt his muscles tense as he looked over her head to the man who'd walked up behind them.

As she stood perfectly still, unable to move, Sheriff Kinkaid walked across the street. She pleaded with her eyes for him to come over and almost cried with relief as she realized he was already heading toward them.

"Everything all right over here, gentlemen?" His voice indicated he already knew there was trouble brewing.

Brooks hadn't moved, making it impossible for her to turn and see Milton behind her. She brought her foot back to the ground and looked up at him. He pulled her closer to him, still not letting her turn, and she was now so close she could feel his chest moving as he breathed.

Her own heart quickened as she realized things were about to take a drastic turn.

"Everything's fine, Sheriff. Just talking to Milton about how Fiona's about to become a blushing bride today," Brooks ground out through clenched teeth.

Her breath caught in her throat as she sucked it in. What was he saying? Was he about to just let Milton take her? Lydia gasped and the wagon lurched as she stood up to come down beside her friend.

The sound of Milton's laughter behind her made her stomach churn.

Apparently, Sheriff Lewis was just as surprised as he stopped beside them and raised an eyebrow in Brooks' direction.

"Can you perform a wedding ceremony, Sheriff?" Brooks still hadn't moved a muscle and the world around her started to spin. He was going to let Milton marry her right here and now.

"I can but are you sure we shouldn't wait a bit and see what other options we have?" Sheriff Kinkaid moved between the two men and her.

Brooks let go of her arm and placed his hands on her shoulders, turning her to face the Sheriff and Milton. Lydia had gotten down and raced over to stand beside her, glaring at her brother.

"How dare you!" She tried to pry his hands from Fiona's shoulders.

"Lydia, step out of the way."

Fiona felt Brooks pushing her toward the Sheriff. She tried to turn away from his grasp, hoping she could make an escape.

His hands wouldn't let go.

Sheriff Kinkaid offered her a kind smile but she couldn't return it. There had to be something he could do to help her, instead of just standing here watching it happen.

Milton was still laughing, the sound piercing her heart with every beat.

The Sheriff nodded at Brooks, then stepped directly in front of Milton, facing her and Brooks.

"Brooks Vaughn, do you take this woman, Fiona Murphy, to be your wife?"

CHAPTER 13

The world around her spun out of control. This wasn't happening. She heard Milton hollering from what seemed like far away as Brooks stared down at her, telling her by the look in his eyes that she needed to say the words that would bind her to him for life.

His grip tightened on her arm as they all waited for her to repeat the words back to the Sheriff.

"I do," her voice came out barely above a whisper. She could barely catch her breath as she looked up into Brooks' face. She thought she saw him give a brief smile but it was gone as fast as it had come. In its place, was the rigid jaw he showed when he was angry.

"You may kiss the bride."

The words broke through the humming she was feeling in her head. Between Milton's yelling, Lydia's

69

gasps, and her own confusion of what was happening, she'd barely heard a word.

But she heard those words.

Brooks winked, then brought his lips down to hers. She vaguely heard Milton in the background but as soon as Brooks' mouth met hers, she couldn't hear anything. He kissed her gently with just a subtle brush of their lips but where they'd touched, she could still feel them burning.

"No! No you don't. She's mine. I paid for her and she's not marryin' anyone but me."

Milton was shoving at the Sheriff's back, who turned to grab hold of the man's arms.

"Hayward, listen here. I'm an officer of the law and I've just bound these two together in marriage. Whether you like it or not, it's no matter to me. But in the eyes of the law, they're now married, so you can't do anything about it. I suggest you turn around and head home."

Milton's face was purple—with eyes bulging from their sockets and his greasy hair hanging down in disarray around his face—his face was crazed. As he set his eyes in her direction, a chill went down her spine.

He wasn't letting her go that easily.

"Get yer hands off me. I paid good money to get that woman out here. She isn't going anywhere else but home with me. I don't care if she's married or not." Milton was nearly frothing at the mouth with blind rage.

He kept pushing forward, trying to get to her.

"I don't take kindly to a man making threats against my wife, Milton. I'd suggest you listen to the Sheriff here and get as far away from me as you can. Because if you dare threaten Fiona, or any other woman, like you have been since she arrived in town, you'll answer to me once and for all."

Brooks pushed her behind him and walked over to help the Sheriff restrain Milton, whose shoulders heaved up and down as the anger consumed him with every breath. His eyes were glossy and his skin had started to mottle with shades of red and purple. Spit flew from his mouth as he sneered in her direction.

"I ain't finished with ye yet. Don't ye think I am." The sheriff and Brooks both pushed him away at the same time, leaving him in a heap on the ground. He never took his eyes off her as he fumbled around on the ground.

Brooks bent down and grabbed him by the scruff of his shirt, dragging him back up to his feet. He pulled the man in close and Fiona watched as he lifted Milton off the ground until he was barely touching it.

"You are finished with her. I'll get you the money you're owed for her ticket out here and you are never to come within spitting distance of her again. Do I make myself clear?"

Brooks' voice rumbled loudly and the crowd that had gathered on the street to watch the production parted to let him drag Milton away from her. When he set him back on his feet, the men stood glaring at each other, neither of them willing to back down.

"Ye'll get what's comin' to ye, Brooks. Ye had no right steppin' in where ye didn't belong."

"That's where you're wrong, Hayward. You let go of any rights you may have falsely believed you had to her the second you used her as payment on a wager. So the way I see it, you gambled and you lost."

Milton squinted his eyes together, frantically looking around at the crowd that had gathered.

Lydia took her hand and pulled Fiona with her, walking behind the wagon as Sheriff Kinkaid kept his eyes on the two men facing off in the street.

Fiona pulled at Lydia, refusing to walk away knowing she was the reason Brooks was having to square off against Milton in the first place.

As she pulled free of Lydia, Milton turned to walk away. She let the breath go she'd been holding as Brooks finally turned to walk back toward them. His eyes met hers and she could see how dangerous he could be if someone crossed him. He had a steely gaze that never wavered and, for a split second, she almost felt sorry for Milton. He hadn't stood a chance against Brooks.

Someone screamed and she whipped her head around to see where it had come from. She caught a brief glimpse of something reflecting the sunlight from Milton's direction. Her mouth moved into an "O" shape and her head swung around to shout a warning to Brooks.

But the shot rang out before she could make a sound and she watched in horror as Brooks fell to the ground clutching at his side.

She started to run but someone from the crowd grabbed both her and Lydia while Sheriff Kinkaid tackled Milton and wrestled him to the ground.

Once it was safe, she was released and ran to where Brooks lay on the dust in the street, a pool of red gathering on the ground beneath him.

Lydia grabbed his arm as she screamed his name. "Brooks! Please, Brooks, you can't leave me. You're all I have!"

Fiona's heart broke with every word her friend cried.

Brooks opened his eyes and offered his sister a weak smile. "It'll take more than a bullet to slow me down, sis." His words were raspy and as he spoke, he coughed, grasping his side in pain.

He turned his eyes to Fiona. She realized she hadn't spoken a word since they'd been married. He swallowed painfully and his eyes clenched shut briefly. When he opened them again, he winked at her again. He took her hand she'd placed on his chest as she'd fallen on her knees beside him. He gently tugged her closer so she could hear his voice, barely loud enough to be heard with the screams around them.

"No matter what happens, you're my wife now, so you're safe. He can't get you now."

CHAPTER 14

T he sound of whispered voices reached his ears through a fog. Something felt heavy on his chest, making it difficult for him to breathe. He tried to open his eyes but pain shot through his forehead making him squeeze them tightly closed again.

He felt like he'd spent too long in the saloon yesterday.

"Are you awake, Brooks?"

The sound of his sister's worried voice broke through the haze. He peeked one eye open and fought to focus on his surroundings. He could see he was in the doctor's office, a place he'd had the misfortune to spend time in on more than one occasion. Usually, after a brawl over a game of cards or even having a bullet wound fixed up once or twice.

Bullet wound.

Now he remembered.

He groaned as he realized even though he'd had a few nicks with a bullet in the past, he'd never really had one in the back like he had now. No wonder he felt so awful.

He vaguely remembered being carried over to the doctor's office by a couple of men who'd been standing on the street while Lewis took care of hauling Milton over to his office.

By the time he'd been laid out on the table and someone had gone to find the doctor who Brooks was sure would have already been drinking since noon, he'd almost passed out from the pain.

But the look of fear on both his sister and Fiona's face had forced him to let on that he was fine.

The terror in Fiona's eyes, as she'd leaned over him on the ground by the street, had filled him with a feeling he couldn't quite understand. He knew Lydia cared about him and he was pretty sure Lewis Kinkaid would possibly be a bit upset if he were to die.

But Fiona didn't have to care one way or another. However, the anguish on her face as she sobbed over him lying in the dirt had shown him she did care, at least a bit. It'd been a long time since a woman had genuinely cared about him and it had warmed something in his heart he'd thought had died long ago.

He tried to turn his head to see where Fiona was now. He felt the need to let her know he was all right, even if he didn't know whether or not that was true.

The movement made the room spin around him. He tried to open his mouth to speak but he felt like he had a wad of cotton in his mouth.

"Brooks! Thank goodness you're awake. I was so worried." Lydia came over beside him, reaching out and grabbing his hand. The movement caused a jarring pain in his side.

The doctor came into his view, looking down at him while shaking his head. "Well, Brooks, I'm starting to think you enjoy my hospitality just a bit too much." The short man laughed at his own joke, the redness in his face standing out against the whites of his eyes. One of the man's eyes was a bright purple color and he suddenly remembered the moment they'd had to take the bullet out of his side.

The men who'd carried him inside, along with Lewis who'd gotten back from locking Milton up, had been instructed to hold him down when Dr. Hastings had arrived. The doctor had been down at the Alamo Saloon and, luckily, he'd brought a bottle of whiskey with him.

Brooks knew now why his head felt like he'd been drinking all day. The men had made him drink as much of the whiskey as he could while the doctor washed up and had gotten the equipment he'd needed to go after the bullet. They'd all made the women wait out in the other room.

As soon as the doctor had leaned over and poked his finger into his wound, Brooks had felt a searing pain unlike any he'd known before. The two men holding him had been no match for him and before anyone had a chance to react, he'd punched the doctor square in the eye and knocked him to the ground.

He didn't remember much after that, so he assumed he'd passed out from the pain.

Brooks finally caught a glimpse of Fiona as she stepped over beside the doctor. Her skin was as white as snow and her hair had almost completely fallen out from the tight bun she'd been wearing it in. It was hanging in tendrils around her shoulders and Brooks had a sudden urge to reach up and run his hands through it.

The look on her face, though, as she glared at the doctor indicated she wouldn't likely appreciate that at the moment. Brooks almost laughed out loud as she stared at the man in shock.

"Dr. Hastings, I'm not sure what you find funny about this situation at all but I'd appreciate if you could keep your jokes to yourself. You may be used to all manner of drunks and lowlifes being brought through your door every day but Mr. Vaughn is neither of those. Now, if you will let us know how he's doing and what we can do to help him heal, we'll take him home with us and provide the care he needs there."

Dr. Hastings was left standing with his jaw hanging open as he stared at the redheaded woman in front of him.

Clearing his throat, he shook his head and turned back to Brooks. "Yes, of course. Well, unfortunately, you lost a great deal of blood. I managed to get the bullet out even after you'd knocked me to the ground."

Fiona spun her head to look at him. Her eyebrows furrowed together. "You hit the doctor?"

He didn't feel like talking yet so he just shrugged his shoulder.

"Yes, ma'am. Your husband gave me this nice shiner here to remember him by." The doctor leaned closer to Fiona and pointed at his bruised eye.

"Oh, he's not my husband. Well, not really." Fiona whipped her eyes back to his with a panic-stricken look.

He almost smiled as she fumbled to explain to the doc.

The doctor looked toward the doorway where Sheriff Kinkaid was walking back into the room. "I thought you said Brooks had married this lady here." He tilted his head at Fiona.

79

"Yes, they're married. She just hasn't had the chance to enjoy the perks of marital bliss yet."

Brooks smiled at the way Fiona was now looking at his friend with narrowed eyes. She wasn't finding any of this amusing.

"Can someone please just let me know if my *husband* is going to live or not? And if he is, what I need to do to make sure he gets better?"

The room went silent as the men all stared at each other, unsure what to say.

"Terribly sorry, Mrs. Vaughn. It's just that this isn't the first time your husband has lain on this table and I guess we've all learned not to take things as serious. Your husband is fine. He lost a lot of blood this time, though, which does concern me. He won't be able to be moved for a while and he's going to have to be careful not to open the wound back up."

The doctor turned to Brooks. "You're gonna be spending some time here with me, I'm afraid. And you won't be doing any work that'll risk opening the wound up and getting infected."

"You're wrong about that. I'm not spending any more time here. I've got a field that needs to come off and I can think of better places I'd rather be on my wedding night than lying on a bed in your dingy office." He tried to sit up, immediately regretting his decision as the pain tore through his side.

His eyes turned to Fiona who stood staring at

him in shock, her mouth hanging slightly open. "It may be our wedding night but, I assure you, there is nothing in our marriage that is real. So, whatever you have in mind, you can forget it. As your *wife*, I will take you home and take care of you until you're better but that's as far as it will go. And if you try anything else, you will find yourself back here lying on this very table before you know what hit you."

Brooks moved his eyes to glare at Dr. Hastings who stood chuckling beside his bed. Letting himself fall back onto the bed, he squeezed his eyes shut. "Maybe you're right, doc. I might be better off staying here with you."

CHAPTER 15

She leaned back against the side of the wagon, trying to get comfortable as it jarred her up and down along the road. Every bounce of the wagon made her suck in her breath as she desperately tried to hold herself still. She hoped Brooks had passed out from the pain she knew he was in. He'd groaned several times since they'd left town.

He had his head and shoulders resting in her lap in the back of the wagon, while Lydia drove back home. She wished she'd known how to handle driving the team pulling the wagon so Lydia could've stayed with her brother in the back. But Fiona thought this was the least she could do to try and help the man who'd taken a bullet because of her.

But as she sat here peeking down at the face of

the man lying with his head in her lap, she struggled with the emotions she was feeling.

The day had been so full of turmoil. She'd realized her father hadn't sent the money she needed, then ended up marrying a man she'd only met because he'd won her in a bet. As if that hadn't been enough to send her world spinning, that same man ended up being shot and almost killed because he'd married her.

Looking down, the lines were etched on the face she was holding in her lap as he clenched his eyes closed in pain again. She wanted to reach down and caress his face to try and ease some of his discomfort but even though, in the eyes of the law, she was his wife, she knew that had little reality in truth.

Unable to stop herself as the wagon jostled over another rock, making Brooks grasp his side in pain, she let her hand gently touch his cheek. As soon as her fingers met the skin on his face, he turned his head slightly to be closer. The lines eased and she thought maybe he'd actually fallen asleep.

She removed her hand in an effort to get more comfortable but he reached up and pulled it back to rest on his cheek. He hadn't even opened his eyes. "Don't move. I'm finally feeling like my insides aren't going to be ripped out with ever blasted bump of this wagon."

His voice sounded strained and she realized just

how much control he was using to hold the pain at bay.

She left her hand on his cheek, feeling the warmth of the skin and the sharpness of the stubble he always wore on his jaw. Her skin tingled where it touched his and she had to fight the urge not to caress his face to give him comfort.

She may be his wife in name but she didn't think she had the right to do that.

Fiona started to feel uncomfortable in the silence with only the squeaking of the old wagon and the sound of the horse's hooves on the road surrounding them. Lydia was having to concentrate hard on driving the wagon, something she didn't have to do often.

"Why didn't you tell me your plan to marry me?" The question had been burning in her mind all day.

Brooks just lay there without moving and she thought he wasn't going to answer. Finally, he opened his eyes and her breath was taken away by the dark amber stare she was looking down at.

"I didn't know if it was going to come to that or not. I'd hoped the money would be there or that we could get out of town without Milton seeing you. But I'd already spoken with Lewis a day or two ago about what other options we had. We decided that if we were backed into a corner, marrying you was our best option."

If he wasn't already in so much pain and she

wasn't feeling so guilty about it all, she might have thrown his head off her lap and stood up. "So, you were backed into a corner? Words I'd always dreamed of hearing my husband say for why he married me."

She knew she was being silly and it shouldn't matter anyway. It was just a marriage to save her from a worse fate, and he'd done it to save her, so she should be thanking him.

But the stress of the day and everything that had happened in the past few hours had left her feeling raw and vulnerable. She looked out at the passing fields and away from the eyes that were looking up at her so he wouldn't notice the wetness that was starting to blur her vision.

"So, now what? Surely we won't have to stay married." She swallowed the lump in her throat. All she'd ever dreamed of was finding a man who could love her for who she was, who could see the woman inside.

She'd come all this way after writing letters to a man who'd made her believe that was possible. Her cheeks burned as she thought about how naive she'd been and what a fool she'd made of herself by doing this.

And now, thanks to her, a stranger was married to her and had been shot because of her decision to come here.

"I hadn't thought that far ahead. Surely you can

tolerate being married to me for a few days at least until we can figure out what to do. Now that Milton's locked up, you should be safe. Once I'm feeling better, we can go back into town and see what the sheriff can do so we can get you back home."

She still couldn't look at him. Why did her heart suddenly feel an ache at the thought of him sending her home now?

His fingers reached up and touched her jaw, pulling her face down to look at him. "We'll get everything worked out, don't worry. I promise, I will get you home where you'll be safe from the ruffians out here, like me." He tried to wink at her again but the pain from moving his arm was obviously too much and he ended up wincing instead.

What would he say if she told him she didn't think she wanted to be safe from the ruffians like him?

CHAPTER 16

His eyes opened and he listened, expecting to hear one of the women in the other room banging around or coming in to fuss over him. He'd managed to hobble in to the house yesterday, leaning on the shoulders of his sister and Fiona, who'd helped support him until he could get to his bed.

He'd never felt so weak before in his life. He'd been in a few scuffles in town and had a couple of bullets scrape him but this was the first time he'd truly been shot. He was angry with himself for even letting it happen. He'd been so distracted and eager to just get Fiona out of town again, he'd turned his back on a man who couldn't be trusted.

That was one of the rules you never broke when you were in a town like Abilene.

Now, he was laid up in his bed while a crop sat in

the field needing to come off. Not to mention the cattle that were depending on him to move them to the other pasture so they could graze before the winter set in.

He sat up, knowing he didn't have the time to be lying around in bed. What did the doctor know anyway? He wasn't much better than he was. Dr. Hastings was a man who had a drinking problem and who couldn't say no to a game of cards. So, just because he had a degree, which Brooks often wondered about the legitimacy of in the first place, it didn't mean he knew what he was talking about.

He ignored the pain that tore through his side and turned to put his legs over the side of the bed. The room was spinning, so he sat for a few minutes until everything slowed down.

He just needed to get up and moving and he'd feel better.

Standing up, he winced as the pain took his breath away. Clutching at his side to support it, he took a step. He limped out to the other room, hunched over to keep his side from hurting as much.

"Lydia?" His voice was raspy, so he cleared his throat and tried again. "Fiona?" He figured since they were now husband and wife, he may as well stop with the formality.

The small house was quiet. They'd been there not too long ago, making him breakfast and fussing over him until he ate something, so he knew they couldn't be far. He must've fallen back asleep. He wondered how long he'd slept.

Moving to the doorway, he pulled it open and staggered out into the hot sunlight. He figured it must be almost midday by the heat in the sun. He lifted his other arm to shield his eyes as he scanned the yard to see where the women could be.

Squinting his eyes as he spotted something in the distance, he cursed to himself as he realized what he was looking at. Fiona lifting the blade to cut the wheat in the field beside the house while Lydia picked it up and placed it in the cart beside her.

He stumbled down the stairs, limping as fast as his legs would take him. He didn't need any help getting this crop off and he sure as blazes wouldn't be letting his sister and new wife do it for him.

He hadn't bothered to put his shirt on, knowing the pain would've been too much to lift his arms. The sun beat down on the bare skin of his back as he moved slowly toward the field.

"Do you ladies mind telling me exactly what you think you are doing out here? I am perfectly capable of taking this crop off myself and I don't need either of you thinking I can't. This is my responsibility and I will do it myself."

Lydia met him as he stumbled into the field. "Brooks, we know you can do it. But right now, you can't. So Fiona thought we should do something to help you until you became well enough to get back out here."

He turned his gaze to Fiona who was standing watching him with her chin in the air, holding the blade in front of her as she leaned on it. She raised her eyebrow as she tilted her head to the side.

"Do you honestly think you could lift this blade and cut the field yourself at the moment?"

He was still clutching his side, trying to ignore the pain that was throbbing with every beat of his heart.

"You have helped me since the day I arrived in town. It might not always have been the kind of help I'd have liked but you helped just the same. And now, like it or not, I'm your wife. And until the law says otherwise, you're stuck with me. As your wife, I'm telling you I'm taking as much of this crop off as I can."

Brooks didn't know what to say. The look she was sending his way wasn't leaving a whole lot of room for argument.

The two of them stood staring at each other in the hot sun, with the dust of the field swirling around them. Slowly walking over to her, he took his free hand and reached out to take the blade from her hand.

"As my *wife*, you are obligated to listen to me. And

I say you're not going to spend another minute out here in this field. Do I make myself clear?" He didn't know why he was so angry about her wanting to help him. His pride stung, knowing he should be the one out here sweating in the field, not these two women.

He wasn't usually an unreasonable man. He knew when he couldn't do something and was normally able to accept the things he couldn't control. But for some reason, seeing Fiona standing out in this field, covered in dirt and sweat, ate at him.

She was used to wearing silks and lace. She shouldn't be wearing a tattered old dress that belonged to his sister.

She should be sitting and drinking tea with her suitors who would be wearing the finest coats their tailors could make them. Instead, she was standing out in a dusty field holding a blade that likely weighed more than her, making sure the crop that would provide for his family was taken off the ground.

She narrowed her eyes as she held the blade firmly in her hand, not letting him pull it out of her grasp.

Finally, she let go of the blade and gave her shoulders a subtle shrug. "Fine. I will obey you, *husband*. You don't mind if I just stand here and watch you for a while, do you?" She crossed her arms in front of her and backed up so he could have the room to work.

He clenched his jaw tightly. She knew he wasn't going to be able to lift this blade and she was standing there watching to make sure he had no choice.

He wasn't backing down that easily.

Letting go of his side he'd been holding, he lifted the blade with both hands. As soon as it moved, he felt a ripping in his side and knew the moment it started bleeding again.

He felt the blade drop to the ground as Fiona gasped. She ran toward him, putting her hands out to him. He fought against the swirling of the movement in his head but he knew he wasn't going to be able to keep standing on his own.

Her arms went around him, helping to hold him up. But his weight was too much for her and he fell to his knees on the dirt.

"You stubborn fool! Why couldn't you just let me help you?" Her voice sobbed and as he turned and looked at her, the fear in her eyes was there again as tears streamed down her face. She pressed her hand to his side and when he looked down, the blood was spreading through her fingers.

His sister was on the other side of him now and both women started tugging on him to stand up. But he had no strength to move and fought hard against the blackness that was threatening.

Watching the tears run down Fiona's cheeks, he wanted to reach out and brush them away, feeling terrible that he'd made her cry.

"I don't need any help." With those words, he knew the blackness had won.

CHAPTER 17

F iona sat at the table, cupping the warm cup of tea in her hands. She didn't think she had any more tears left to shed, so she sat staring blankly out the window at the field she could still see blowing in the wind.

"He'll be all right, Fiona. Brooks is a fighter. He's never backed down from anything and this will be no different." Lydia's voice reached her ears and she turned her head to offer a weak smile for her friend. She knew she was worried too, so she reached over and placed her hand on hers.

"I know, Lydia. It's just..." She choked on a sob she hadn't realized was so close to the surface. Swallowing hard, she waited to continue. "It's just that the past few weeks have been so trying. And now your brother is lying in there fighting for his life because of me. I just feel so helpless." She shook her head.

"Why couldn't he have just stayed in his bed? Why does he have to be so stubborn? If we want to take that field off, then that's exactly what we're going to do. And now he won't have any say in it one way or another."

They'd managed to get him up on the cart they had out in the field to pile the wheat on and had practically dragged him back to the house after he'd lost consciousness. Thankfully, as they got closer to the house, Sheriff Kinkaid had been riding up the lane. He helped them get him into the house, then rode back to town for the doctor.

She'd tried to nurse his wound that was bleeding badly while they waited for the doctor but she worried it hadn't been enough.

The doctor was in there now, trying to fix the damage he'd done by lifting the blade. She felt the weight of guilt even more than before, knowing she'd goaded him into doing it, determined to prove he couldn't.

Hearing the door open, she jumped up from her chair and spun to face the doctor and sheriff who'd come out of the room.

"He's one stubborn cuss, that's for sure." The doctor was shaking his head. "He tried to hit me again!" He looked at the women, hoping for some kind of sympathy.

"Does that mean he's awake?" She couldn't keep the hope from her voice, ignoring the look she got from the doctor for not acknowledging the assault he'd almost endured.

"Hmph...well, he was. But he's not now."

Sheriff Kinkaid moved past the doctor and walked over to where they stood by the table. "What the doctor is saying, is that he had to stitch the wound back up. While Brooks woke up briefly during the ordeal to take a swing at the fine doctor here, he promptly lost consciousness again before he could do more damage to his face."

He looked at Fiona. "What was he doing out of bed?"

She swallowed, feeling a sense of protectiveness. "He was insistent he could work in the field when he saw us out there cutting the wheat." She lifted her eyes to his. "You know how stubborn he can be."

The sheriff grinned, then nodded his head. "Yes, that he is. I reckon seeing you ladies out working in that field was enough to send him right over the edge."

"Well, he's going to pay for his stubbornness." The doctor wanted to make sure they were listening to him as he walked over beside the sheriff. "He'd already lost a lot of blood. Now he's going to have an even harder fight to come back from this. I'm afraid it's not looking good for him, especially if an infection sets in."

Fiona felt her heart drop to her stomach. What did he mean, it wasn't looking good for him?

"Doctor, what can we do? How will we know if he gets an infection?" She had to do something.

The doctor just shook his head. "It depends on him. If you have to, tie him down so he can't get out of that bed. And if an infection sets in, you'll know. About all you can do then is pray."

"Doc, you don't need to be scaring the ladies like that," the sheriff sternly scolded the doctor as he shook his head. He turned back to look at them. "Brooks will be fine. I've never known anyone as hotheaded as that man in there. He isn't going to let a bullet wound take him down."

Fiona knew he was only trying to make them feel better, but the doctor's words kept going around in her mind. What if he did get an infection? Could she and Lydia care for him enough to get him through it?

She turned to her friend who looked like the world had dropped out from beneath her. Thanks to her, Lydia could possibly lose the only family she had left. She went over and put her arms around her, offering her what she could for comfort.

"I'll take the doc back into town, then I'll come back out and check on you all a little later. I was going to let you all know that the judge will be in town in a week's time to deal with Milton. That's what I'd been coming out to tell you. Until then, he'll be locked up in the cell in my office, so you'll be safe from him."

"Thank you, Sheriff Kinkaid." Her voice trembled as she fought the tears that were threatening.

"Call me Lewis. Brooks is my friend and, since you're his wife, I'd expect we'd be friends too." He offered her a kind smile.

"Am I really his wife? I don't even know anymore what's real and what isn't. Everything these past few days has been so overwhelming, I feel like I don't even know where I am anymore." She let her hands drop from Lydia's shoulders and moved to sit down in the chair she'd been sitting in earlier.

The sheriff walked over, placing his hand on her shoulder. "You're his wife, have no doubt about that. He wanted to make sure Milton couldn't do anything to you and he figured having you married to him would give him more power with the law to protect you."

She lifted her eyes to look at the sheriff. "But why? Why would he bother to do that for a stranger?" She still didn't understand why he'd gone to the trouble of marrying her just to save her from Milton.

"I'd reckon that's a question you'd do better to

ask Brooks yourself." The sheriff smiled, then turned to head out with the doctor.

She sat watching them go and tried to ignore the niggling voice in her head that said she might never get the chance to ask him herself.

CHAPTER 18

He opened his eyes, finally feeling like his head wasn't on fire for the first time in days. He was scared to move in case he ended up having the sickness come rushing back at him.

He could remember bits and pieces from the last few days and he knew there were moments he'd just wished he would die. But every time he felt like that, he'd see the pale face of the woman who'd been sitting at his bedside, placing the cold cloths on his head. She'd changed the sheets as he thrashed about in his sweat from fever and desperately kept trying to get water into his mouth when he was awake enough to try.

His sister had been there too, and he hated to think about what worry she'd been going through. He'd heard her crying through the fog in his brain and he'd tried so hard to let her know he was all right.

Now, though, she sat beside his bed looking out the window. "Hey, sis. How come you look so pitiful?"

He smiled as she jumped up, whipping her head around to look at him. "You're awake! Brooks, I swear you've taken about ten years off my life worrying about you these past few days." She tried to be stern but he could see the relief on her face as she looked down on him.

Her brown hair hung around her face and, as he looked at her, he realized she wasn't a little girl anymore. She was a beautiful woman and he wished there was a man out there who could see past her limp for the woman she was inside.

She moved to sit on the edge of the bed and he lifted his hand to take hers. His hand felt like it had a piece of lead tied to it as he moved it, shocking him at his weakness.

"Careful. I don't need this tearing open again." She pulled back a bit to make sure she didn't bump him as she sat down.

"Well in fairness, it wouldn't have torn open in the first place if you'd listened and just stayed in your bed like you'd been told to."

He'd only been awake a minute and she was already scolding him.

"I've never been particularly good at taking

orders. You may have noticed." He grinned, knowing how irritated it would make her.

"Yes, I have noticed. And because of it, you almost died."

He was starting to see she wasn't in a joking mood.

Closing his eyes, he sighed to himself. "I wasn't going to die. You know I'm too stubborn for that."

"Do you know the guilt poor Fiona has been feeling since you were shot? Do you have any idea what she's been going through?"

He opened his eyes back up as he heard the anger in his sister's voice.

"What is she feeling guilty about? Other than the fact that she couldn't listen and just leave the field to me, she hasn't done anything wrong."

Lydia shook her head and scrunched her eyebrows together. "Are you really that thickheaded, Brooks? That girl left her family behind to come out here hoping for a better life, based on the lies of that slime Milton Hayward. Only to end up being passed off to a stranger over a wager at cards, then dragged out to his house without any idea of what would happen to her when she arrived."

Lydia stood up, apparently ready to tell him exactly what was on her mind. "Then her father didn't come through with the money she needed to get back home. It was hard enough for her pride to even have to go begging for it and she ends up married to the man who won her before she even has a chance to understand what was going on. She was never given any say in the matter, only being told it was to keep her safe."

His sister was riled, so he closed his eyes and let her finish.

"When you got shot, she blamed herself because she said you wouldn't have been in danger if not for her. That's why she wanted to help you take your field off. And that's why she's sat at your bedside, holding cloths on your thick head while you thrashed and got sick all over her. That's why she's been sitting in here crying, when she didn't think any of us could hear her."

Fiona had been crying at his bedside too?

"And you brush it off like it's no big deal. Like you weren't really that badly off anyway. She's carrying the guilt of everything you've done to help her. And you won't even let her help you in return, without being a stubborn oaf who can't listen to simple orders and stay in your bed."

He peeked one eye open and Lydia's arms were crossed, looking down at him.

"Are you finished?" He didn't want to interrupt if she felt she had more to say.

She bent down closer to him and pointed her finger at his chest. "You will not say one word in argument when you find out she's been working in the field with me while you were sick. We took turns while one stayed in the house to look after you and now it's almost finished."

He clenched his teeth together. "Why am I not surprised?"

She stood back up straight, glaring down at him. "While I'm happy to see that you're through the worst of it, I have to consider my friend's feelings too. She's become my closest friend in the world and I hate seeing the worry she's been feeling. Not to mention the confusion she feels over whether she's supposed to be your wife or not."

He raised an eyebrow. "What's that supposed to mean? I married her, didn't I?"

He watched as she slowly shook her head and rolled her eyes. "You married her to keep her safe. And now she doesn't quite know what her role is supposed to be. She knows it wasn't a marriage out of love. Have you thought about what you're going to do now, about your marriage?"

It was his turn to roll his eyes. "In case you hadn't noticed, Lydia, I've been a bit busy since saying my vows." He didn't want to admit that in the moments of lucidity he'd had over the past few days, that was all he could think about.

Hearing the door open, they both turned their heads and Fiona came into the room. Her hair was hanging all around her shoulders, seeming to never be able to stay up in the clips she tried to tie it up with. Her face was smudged with dirt and her hands were black. He saw her try to wipe them on her skirt as she rushed toward him.

"Brooks! Thank goodness you're awake."

"He just woke up. I was going to come and let you know." Lydia smiled down at him. "Now I'm going to go get dinner ready. You two have a lot to talk about I'm sure."

Glaring at his sister's retreating back, he wished he had the strength to throw something at it before she made it through the door.

CHAPTER 19

"I should have a wash. I must look a mess." Fiona stood beside the bed, reaching up and patting at the loose curls that hung around her face. She didn't know if it was going to make any difference or not but the silence in the room as he stared at her was unnerving.

"You look fine." He moved his arms under himself to try sitting up, wincing from the pain, so she moved over and bent down to help him. Putting her hands under his shoulders, she let him use her strength to pull himself up a bit more on the bed.

She grabbed the pillows and set them up for him to lean back on.

"Thanks," his voice sounded strained.

"You should just lie still and not be moving around yet. You've been through so much these past few days. You don't want to end up opening your wound and risking another infection."

He was just staring at her, making her stomach clench with worry.

"You're surely wondering why I'm covered in dirt when you told me not to go out to do the wheat but someone had to do it. I know you aren't going to be feeling well enough for a while. Besides, I had to pay you back for all your help with Milton. I couldn't just sit here and let your crop die in the field." She knew she was rambling but he still wasn't saying anything and she knew he was going to be angry.

"Thank you."

"And it really wasn't difficult. Lydia and I took turns caring for you while the other would go out and... What did you say?" She stopped talking, bringing her eyebrows together as she looked at him propped on the pillows.

"I said, thank you."

"Oh." Suddenly, unsure what to say, or what to do, she lowered herself down into the chair beside the bed. She'd spent the past few days sitting in it as she'd tried to fight the fever that had Brooks in its grasp.

"Can you hand me that cloth?" He tilted his head toward the basin that was sitting on the table beside his bed. She reached in and wrung the cloth out, handing it to him. Before she could pull her hand back, he'd grabbed onto it, staring down at the dirt that was encrusted into her palms.

Without saying anything, he gently wiped at the dirt, quickly turning the cloth a dark color as the whiteness of her palms started to show through. He lifted his eyes, meeting hers that had been entranced, watching as he wiped her hands clean. "You have some pretty awful looking blisters here. You should put some salve on them."

He handed her the cloth and she turned to put her hands into the basin to finish getting the dirt from them. When she sat back to face him, he lifted his hand and rubbed his thumb under her eye. "You missed a spot."

He gently wiped the dirt from below her eye, never taking his eyes from hers. She felt like she was trapped, the skin beneath his thumb burning wherever he touched.

What was he doing?

"Thank you for taking care of me. I know I caused you some worry but I guess you'll have learned by now, bullet wounds are just a part of life around these parts. Men like me don't usually live long anyway."

"What do you mean, men like you?"

His thumb was making slow circles on her cheek and she was finding it difficult to concentrate on what he was saying.

He laughed quietly. "A man doesn't get shot by

sitting in church, Fiona. Since this isn't the first time I've been on the receiving end of a gun fight, I'd figure you'd be running for the hills by now to get away from the ruffian you married."

She grabbed his hand, forcing him to stop the caressing that was making her heart feel like it was about to beat out of her chest.

"You're not a ruffian, Mr. Vaughn. A ruffian wouldn't do what you've done to help a woman. You could have taken advantage of me, and my situation, but you didn't. So, you can pretend you're a rake and a scoundrel to the men in town but I know the truth."

The amber of his eyes darkened as he watched her. She swallowed, suddenly feeling her throat go dry under his stare.

"You're my wife now. You can call me Brooks."

She didn't feel like a wife but even she had to admit it felt strange to still address him so formally.

He still hadn't moved his eyes from her face.

"So, Milton's locked up now. I'd reckon you're safe from him."

He brought his hand back down and she felt a coldness take the place where his fingers had been. All she could do was nod.

"We can see what our options are when I'm well enough to head into town. You'll want to head home once your money gets here from your father, so we'll ask Lewis what we can do for an annulment."

Her chest felt like it was suddenly heavy, making it difficult to breathe. The thought of going back to London, back to the insincerity of the people who only cared about the status of others made her heart sick.

She missed her father and her sisters, terribly. But she didn't want to go back to living the shallow life she'd been forced to endure.

Out here, she felt free. Even though she had to work her fingers raw to survive, she felt alive and useful. Here, she felt like she had a purpose.

And no one made her feel like she was less than what she was because of a mark on her skin that made her look a bit different than everyone else.

She realized she'd reached up and pulled at her blouse, something she hadn't worried about doing for days. Her eyes met Brooks' as he lifted his hand again to pull hers away from her neck.

"Why do you do that?"

He spoke the words quietly, his eyebrows furrowed and his head tilted slightly.

She shrugged. "I don't realize I'm doing it. It's just easier to keep it covered than to deal with people asking me about it or turning away when they see the mark."

He shook his head. "Well don't. Don't ever try to cover it up around me." He still held her hand that he'd pulled down, covering it with his own on the bed.

She sat, caught in his stare, sure he was going to say something more. She found herself secretly begging for him to say she was beautiful and that he wanted her to stay here with him.

What had gotten into her?

Hearing the door open behind her, she let go of the breath she'd been holding. She moved to stand up but Brooks held her hand firmly beneath his.

"I brought you some stew, Brooks, so you better get eating and build some of your strength back up." Lydia's voice broke the spell and Fiona pulled her hand away from his, jumping up to move away from the bed.

"I'll be back in to check on you in a while. I'm going to have a wash before dinner." She tried not to let on she was running from the room but she almost ran into Lydia who was holding the tray full of hot, nourishing food at the end of the bed.

As she made her way out the door, Brooks' voice reached her ears. "Great timing, sis."

CHAPTER 20

T he sounds of the early night closed around her as she drank her tea. A wolf could be heard crying in the distance, the sound echoing the feeling in her heart. It was a sad sound, like a lost soul calling out for someone to find them.

She'd only been in Kansas about a month but she already felt more at home here than she ever had in London.

She sat on the step, allowing the breeze to gently kiss her face as she lifted it to the sky and letting her eyes close as she breathed in the freshness of the air. Everything was so clean here. Dustier than London but so much cleaner.

Lydia had gone to bed early, the exhaustion of looking after Brooks and working in the field leaving her unable to stay awake any longer. Fiona was tired too but she knew she wouldn't be able to sleep. She was feeling so confused, unsure what she wanted or even where she wanted to be anymore.

Four months ago, she'd been so excited to get away from London and come out here. A month ago, when she'd arrived and saw firsthand the crude civilization out here that would have a man placing a wager for a woman, she'd wanted to turn around and head as far away from here as she could get.

But now she dreaded leaving here. And she was willing to admit that perhaps it was for more reasons than the scenery and fresh air.

Brooks was never the kind of man she'd thought she'd be drawn to but somehow, during the time she'd been here, she found herself imagining what life could be like if they were married for real.

Her cheeks burned as she remembered the day he'd woken up. When he'd stroked her cheek so tenderly, she'd almost believed he could possibly have feelings for her too. And when he'd told her not to cover up her mark on her neck, her heart had done a somersault as she let herself imagine he thought she was beautiful.

Brooks was a different man than the men back home and she wondered if that was what appealed to her. He'd been brash and unfeeling when he'd dragged her onto his horse the first day they'd met and, in truth, she would never have thought she could care for a man so uncivilized at that time.

But he'd shown her so many times the kind of

man he truly was beneath the hard exterior he put on for the world to see.

"Dreaming about the ballrooms in London?" His voice startled her, making her spill the tea onto her lap as she flung her head forward at the unexpected sound. She'd been so caught up in her thoughts, enjoying the solitude of the night that she hadn't even heard him open the door and come out onto the porch.

"Brooks, you startled me." She dabbed at her skirt as he came over, slowly lowering himself down beside her. She watched as he held tightly to the rail beside him to help ease himself onto the step. He'd started to heal over the past few days but she knew he still had a long way to go.

"Sorry, didn't mean to sneak up on you. I thought you'd heard me calling you when I got up and went into the kitchen looking for you."

"No, I was just enjoying the quiet. I knew I wouldn't be able to sleep yet, so I thought I'd stay out here so I didn't keep you or Lydia awake. I was lost in my thoughts and didn't hear you. Do you need something?" She felt bad, knowing she should have been in the house if he needed her for something.

He sighed. "Fiona, I'm perfectly fine now. You and Lydia don't need to keep fussing over me. It's been a week since I got the bullet in my back and I've been able to get up and move around on my own just fine the past couple of days. I'm going to go crazy if I have to spend another day stuck in bed having you two women fluffing my pillows or coming running at the slightest cough."

"Well, I seem to remember you saying the same thing only a few days ago and that landed you flat on your back fighting a fever that threatened to kill you. So you'll have to excuse us if we have a hard time believing you are as fine as you say you are."

She smiled to herself as he at least had the decency to look sheepish at her mention of what happened last time.

"Well I'm better now."

They sat quietly for a moment, listening to the sound of the creek trickling behind the house. Frogs could be heard doing their nightly calls and the sound of a lone owl softly hooted.

"We have to head in to town tomorrow. The judge will be here and I want to make sure Milton won't be getting free any time soon." He sat with his elbows resting on his legs, leaning forward to avoid pulling anything on his side. He turned his head to look at her.

"You can head up to the wire office while I take care of all that. See if your father has sent your money yet."

Her heart lurched at the mention of receiving money to go home.

He looked out past the barn into the darkness of

the night. "I'll talk to Lewis while I'm there and see what we can do about our marriage."

She swallowed hard, unable to form a word.

"I guess I should've thought things through a bit more. I didn't really put much thought into how we'd get out of it. At the time, I thought it'd be the best way to keep you safe from that leech, Milton. It shouldn't be too difficult to have it annulled since we haven't been married long and haven't shared a bed."

When he casually mentioned them not having shared a bed, she'd sucked the air in too fast and she now sat sputtering unceremoniously on the step beside him.

When she got herself back under control, he was grinning. He'd purposely wanted to shock her and was enjoying the reaction she had.

"We better head in and get some sleep. It could be a long day tomorrow." He pushed himself up, then leaned against the rail to help him step up. He put his hand out for hers.

She could see his eyes in the glow of the moonlight and the lantern that she'd hung on the post outside the door when she'd come outside. His eyes never wavered, daring her to refuse his hand. She wanted to slip her fingers into his palm and never let go.

Reaching her hand up to take his, her skin blazed with heat the moment she touched him. As she stood, she fought against the shakiness of her legs that threatened to give out beneath her. She stepped up to the step he was on and when she was alongside him, he tugged her gently toward him.

He held her hand in front of him, reaching up with his other to push the stray pieces of her hair that hung loosely back behind her ear. Everywhere he touched left a trail of fire and as she looked up at his face, he was watching every movement of his hand.

He kept moving his fingers, softly touching her skin across her cheek and down her jawline until he came to the spot where her birthmark tore across her skin. Instead of turning away, he let his hand gently move over it. She knew he'd soon feel the parts that were raised from the skin and she automatically tried to pull backward from his touch, not wanting him to feel repulsed.

He moved his gaze to hers and gently shook his head. The hand he still held in his wasn't letting her move.

"Stop. I've told you not to try covering this anymore. You're a beautiful woman, Fiona, and this mark doesn't take anything away from that. Anyone who thinks otherwise is a fool."

He kept his hand trailing down, following the line of redness that made its way down her neck. She swallowed and had to lick her lips against the sudden dryness she was feeling.

His eyes watched her every movement and before she knew what was happening, his head was coming toward her and his lips were on hers. His hand still made the tender movements along her neck, caressing up and down to her jaw as she stood unable to move.

His lips pushed hers open, softly asking for permission. His other hand let go of hers and he threaded his fingers up into her hair at the back, gently pulling her head in closer.

As he kissed her, her body tingled. Everywhere he touched sent shivers down her spine. His lips moved on hers, while his fingers continued their assault on her senses, sliding around to the front of her neck.

When he pulled his head back, his eyes were almost black as they looked down into hers. Her lips felt swollen and she realized, at some point, she'd leaned in on him and now her entire body was pressed against his.

"I wish I could give you more, Fiona. You deserve the finest ball gowns and a man who doesn't spend his days sitting in dusty saloons, playing cards against the lowest of crooks and miscreants. You don't want to be tied to a man who most likely hasn't seen his last bullet."

"Brooks, stop! I don't like hearing you talk like that. You know, you always try to act like you're this no-good ruffian who's no better than the cheaters you play against. But I know that's not true. You could stop gambling, stop going to the saloons any time, but you aren't prepared to give up the thirst you have for revenge so you can see that you aren't like those men. You aren't like them."

His eyes creased as he watched her.

She felt something in him change as he stood up straight, setting her gently away from him. "Who told you I'm out for revenge?"

She inwardly cringed, knowing she'd slipped up, telling him something his sister had told her in confidence. Her mind had been so muddled, lost in the moment, and she hadn't been thinking straight.

She couldn't meet his eyes. Pushing herself away from him, she wiped at her skirt with trembling hands, before turning to go in the house. She stopped and turned back, he was silhouetted in the light of the moon.

"You can make your own choices, Brooks. You're a grown man. But you could find that someday, when you're ready to be the man you truly are, it might be too late."

She turned back around and went inside, closing the door behind her. She had to put some distance between her and the man she just realized she'd fallen in love with.

CHAPTER 21

"So what are you going to do?"

Brooks looked down at the papers he held in his hand, wishing he knew the answer. Lewis had managed to get annulment papers drawn up while the judge was here and now he was wishing he'd never even mentioned it.

He'd secretly thought maybe it would take a long time, which the judge had said it sometimes did. But since he was here, he was happy to oblige already. He'd been told why Brooks had married Fiona and he said he felt it was a noble reason but that the two of them shouldn't be bound in a marriage neither of them wanted.

"Well I have no doubt Fiona will be on the first ship back to London as soon as she can get these papers signed but I'm going to leave it up to her to sign them first. If she signs, then I'll sign them too.

I've grown fond of her and would be able to consider making ours a real marriage if not for the fact that I'm not ready to be the man she deserves to be married to."

"Fond of her? Who are you trying to kid, Brooks? I'm not a simpleton who can't even see what's going on in front of him. You've been smitten with that girl since the moment you saw her in the saloon. You can deny it all you want, But I'm not buying it. While I know you're not the kind of man to leave a woman in distress, I also know you aren't one who'd let himself get married to one unless there was more to it." Sheriff Kinkaid chuckled loudly, making Brooks raise his eyebrow in his direction to show his lack of amusement.

"That's not really the point, Lewis. And if you could stop your snickering long enough to let me continue, it would be appreciated."

"Sorry...continue." The sheriff was leaning back against his desk, with his arms crossed over his chest. The judge had already heard the case against Milton and he was being prepared to be taken to Topeka to spend some time in jail. Brooks couldn't see that man taken away fast enough.

He'd still been hollering that he'd never gotten the money owed to him and that Brooks had cheated him but no one was even listening to him at that point.

Now that he was no longer a threat though, it

left Brooks with the task of deciding what to do with his marriage. He thought if he were to ask her, Fiona would most likely be willing to stay. He could see she wouldn't find the idea completely distasteful.

But he also wasn't ready to let go of the burning desire for revenge that had consumed him these past years.

And that meant, he had to let Fiona make the choice herself whether or not she should go back to London where she could be happy and find someone who was more worthy of her or stay here with him.

"The point I'm trying to make, is that Fiona grew up near London, where she didn't have to dig in the dirt of a garden to get her food. She never had to carry a blade heavier than her to cut down a wheat field while the man who should have been taking care of her was laid up in bed from a gunshot wound. Can you see my point?"

Lewis just lifted his eyebrow and shrugged. "Doesn't seem to me like she minds it too much. In fact, if you ask me, she looks happier and healthier than she did when she first arrived in town."

Brooks stood up and tossed the papers he was holding on the desk. "I don't have time to stand around here talking to you when you aren't prepared to listen." He was in a foul mood, not getting much sleep last night after he went back inside the house.

All he could think about were the soft, warm lips that had been under his. And how she'd leaned into him, setting his whole body on fire. If she hadn't mentioned his thirst for revenge, which had been like cold water thrown on his face, he was sure he would've dealt with the pain that would be sure to come, and carried her to his bed.

But when he realized she'd been talking with his sister and they both thought he was only after revenge, he'd been angry. He didn't care what people thought about his decisions, or why he did what he did, but for some reason hearing Fiona question his choices riled him.

He'd spent his life waiting to take everything away from the man who'd cheated his father. That man had ended up destroying his entire family, costing them more than the money his father lost that day.

Brooks didn't have the time to get distracted by a woman. Especially a woman who couldn't understand his motives.

He walked to the doorway, looking out through the glass in the window to see Fiona coming out of the wire office. She held something in her hands but he couldn't see what it was.

Why did his heart feel like it was being torn in two when he realized it could be the money she needed to get back home?

❦

SHE STOOD ON THE STREET, staring across at the sheriff's office, knowing Brooks was still inside. Her heart raced, still unsure what to do.

She held the wire transfer of money from her father in her hands and all she had to do now was walk to the bank to get the money for her ticket home. There would be a train through tomorrow that could take her back to a port out on the east coast so she could board a ship for England.

The thought of making the trip back the way she'd come made her shudder. It hadn't been easy to get here on her own and she knew it'd be harder to go back.

Her eyes stayed on the office across the street as her mind tried to understand what she should do. She suddenly sensed eyes on her and her body trembled as she realized Brooks was standing in the doorway, looking across at her.

She turned her head and saw Lydia come out of the mercantile down the street. She'd said she'd meet her there after she checked the wire office. Since she hadn't expected the message to be there, she hadn't thought she'd be too long.

Lydia smiled and waved as she came toward her holding the few items she'd purchased in her hands.

These two people had become so important to her in the short time she'd been here and she couldn't imagine leaving them. She needed more time to think.

Tucking the papers inside the pocket of her dress, she smiled and waved back at Lydia.

"What took you so long? I thought maybe you'd been accosted out here on the street but I knew Brooks would likely be keeping a close eye on you, so I wasn't too worried."

Fiona smiled at her friend who seemed so much more sure of herself now, walking into the mercantile on her own without worrying what anyone else thought. She loved Lydia dearly, as much as her own sisters back home and was glad to see the redness in her cheeks as she came up beside her.

"No, things were just a bit slow today in the wire office."

"So, still no word from your pa?" Fiona smiled at the term Lydia used for her father.

"No, nothing yet." She felt terrible lying but she couldn't face making any decisions yet. She'd tell her when the time was right.

As they walked across the street to where they'd left the wagon, Brooks came out. Fiona's step faltered as his eyes met hers. Even from there, she could feel the heat in his gaze.

Sheriff Kinkaid walked out behind him, placing his hat on his head as he followed Brooks down the steps.

A man was walking toward the sheriff's office

from the other direction and when he spotted the men on the step, he shouted to them, "I hear ye've got my son locked up in here. You better have a good reason for pressing charges against him or ye'll have me to deal with."

The man's voice raised the hair on the back of her neck. Whoever he was, she didn't want to get any closer. She and Lydia stayed back by the wagon as he kept walking over.

"And who might your son be? We have a few men locked up at the moment."

"Milton Hayward's my son. I've been away for a few years but soon as I heard he was in trouble, I headed back this direction."

Fiona's heart dropped as the man drew up beside them. He had a scar that made its way down his face, stretching from the top of his eye, down to his lip.

This couldn't be a coincidence and she knew the moment Brooks saw the scar, she was right.

He was already striding over to the man, fists clenched at his sides.

"What's your name?" The barely restrained fury in his voice made his voice come out lower than its usual pitch.

The other man spat on the ground before tilting his head and crossing his arms. "Not sure what it is to you, but my name's Virgil. Virgil Hayward."

CHAPTER 22

"Brooks, think this through. You're not being rational," Lydia's voice reached his ears but he couldn't hear anything. All he could hear was the blood rushing in his head at the realization he was about to do the one thing he'd spent his life waiting for.

He was headed to Topeka to sit down for a game of cards with the man who'd ruined his life.

Since they were transporting Milton to the small jail there, Brooks knew Virgil was likely only heading that way to cause trouble over his son but he didn't care. All he could think about was the way the man had laughed in his face when he'd told him he wanted to play him a hand.

But when he told him his name, Virgil had listened. Those years of sitting at the tables had paid off. His name was well known now and no one wanted to pass up the opportunity to try and beat Brooks Vaughn.

Even Virgil Hayward.

He'd told him to meet him in Topeka in two days' time and they'd have their chance to play.

He lifted his head as he shrugged his coat over his shoulders, being careful not to hurt the wound that still ached when he moved too quickly. His eyes met Fiona's across the table where she was sitting.

Her skin had gone as white as it had been when she first arrived in town. She hadn't spoken a word to him on the way home yesterday and when they'd arrived, he'd barely seen her the rest of the day.

He'd been caught up in making sure everything was done so he could leave for a few days without worry. He realized now he'd never spoken to her at all since he'd left Lewis's office in town.

He stood still, watching her face as she looked back at him. Her gaze seemed distant and she was clenching her hands tightly in front of her.

But she still never said a word. He knew she likely had a great deal to say, so he wondered why she was so quiet.

"Fiona, can you please try to talk some sense into him? He won't listen to me. He's not well enough to be riding a day to play cards against a man who's been known to kill men who beat him."

His head swung around to look at his sister.

"Who told you that?"

"Brooks, I'm not a little girl. I can find things out for myself. I know about this man and I know he's dangerous. If you won't listen to me, maybe you'll have the decency to listen to your wife." With those words, she turned and walked out the door, the walls shaking in the small house as the door slammed behind her.

He braced himself for the scolding he knew he was about to face from Fiona as he turned back to her. She still sat quietly watching him, not saying a word.

He walked over to the table and put his hand out for her to stand up. She was making him nervous just sitting there looking at him like that.

"You know I have to do this, right?" He didn't know why he felt the need to explain himself to her. It wasn't like they were truly man and wife.

She stood in front of him and gave him a sad smile. "No, Brooks, I don't. I know you believe you need to do this. But I've told you before, it's your decision. I'm not really in any position to have the right to tell you otherwise."

He brought his hand up to her cheek, tenderly touching the skin and hoping she'd understand. "When I get back, it'll all be over. I'd like to sit down then and talk about things between us. I'd like to see where we can go from here."

He wanted to beg her to just wait until he got home and maybe he could be a true husband to her then. He could give up playing the tables all day and they could work at making a life together.

He knew now how much he desperately wanted her to stay in his life.

But he'd waited too long for this day to walk away from it now.

He bent over, pulling her to him as he crushed her lips under his. This time, she kissed him back with abandon, giving him so much hope for their future. He held her body close to him, feeling her arms go around his back as she held him to her.

When he finally pulled back, her cheeks were red and her eyes were glazed as she looked up at him.

He held her, his face so close to hers he could feel her breath on his skin. "I'll only be gone a couple of days. After that, we can make this a real marriage. If that's what you want."

His heart raced, as he stared down into the green eyes peering back up at him. She reached up and placed her hand on his cheek, softly caressing his skin. He closed his eyes, letting himself feel the heat as he pushed his face toward her touch.

"Be careful, Brooks."

All he could do was nod as he pulled away, taking her hand and placing a kiss on her fingers.

"You can bet on it."

CHAPTER 23

The whistle of the train echoed in her ears, her heart suddenly feeling like it was being squeezed as the realization hit her she would soon be on a ship heading across the ocean and back home.

Away from Brooks.

It felt like it was only a few days since she'd been on the train headed in the other direction, so full of hope and excitement for her future with a man she could fall in love with and who could possibly love her in return.

How wrong she'd been.

She'd found a man to love but she knew now he couldn't be the man who would love her back. His need for revenge had been all consuming and he'd chosen to go against the wishes of everyone who believed he was putting himself in harm's way by playing against Virgil.

Sheriff Kinkaid had told him not to do it. Lydia had pleaded with him not to go, telling him he was all she had left in the world. Even Doctor Hastings had told him he was a fool if he went and not to come back to him to fix any damage he suffered as a result.

That's why she hadn't even bothered to ask him not to go. She'd seen the look in his eyes and knew then he had to go. He was risking his life, knowing he could be killed over a game of cards, hoping for revenge that wouldn't change anything anyway.

And she didn't matter enough for him to stay.

She could have asked him, begged him to stay for her, but she couldn't have lived with the pain it would've caused her heart when he left.

So she'd packed everything up and Lydia drove her into town. Saying good-bye to her friend had been hard but she knew if she didn't leave while Brooks was gone, she wouldn't be able to think clearly with him around.

The truth was, he'd stolen her heart and no matter how strong she tried to be, she knew she couldn't leave as long as there was a chance he wanted her to stay.

When she got to town, she'd gone into Sheriff Kinkaid's office and talked to him. He mentioned that Brooks had managed to get an annulment agreement drawn up and had left it up to her to sign it.

She put her signature on it, letting him have his freedom. He'd done enough for her and being tied to a woman wasn't in his plans at the moment. He shouldn't have to suffer because of something she'd caused by coming out here unprepared for what awaited her.

The sheriff had tried to talk her out of it, saying that Brooks would come to his senses soon enough and she should really wait and talk to him first.

The thought of Brooks brought a sob to her throat. For all she knew, he'd already played Virgil and could be lying on the ground with another bullet in him. She fought the urge to jump up and demand the conductor take her back to him. The thought of him lying there hurt, or worse, tore at her heart.

But she also knew it was a choice he'd made.

Now as she saw the station ahead, the tears started to blur her vision. She had to spend the night in a small town just outside of St. Louis before she could catch the train that would take her the rest of the way.

After that, there'd be no turning back.

"You ain't got it in ya," Virgil's voice taunted him across the table.

Brooks was having trouble concentrating and it had nothing to do with the cards he was holding.

There was something in the way Fiona had looked at him when he'd left and told him to be careful. The more time he'd had to think about it, the more he started to believe she'd been saying more than that.

He was starting to think she'd been saying good-bye.

He shook his head, trying to get his head back in the game. They had a lot of money riding on this hand and he knew he needed to concentrate. He'd won the first few hands but he had his suspicions that Virgil was just toying with him, wanting him to have the bigger stakes to throw into the pot.

"Brooks, I think we need to talk." His head flew up as he recognized Lewis's voice.

"Kinkaid, what are you doing here?" He growled at his friend who'd come up behind him. "I'm in the middle of a game. I don't need you distracting me."

Lewis looked down at him and shook his head. "You just don't get it, do you?"

"Get what? Spit it out, Lewis, I need to finish what I've started here."

The sheriff tipped his head in Virgil's direction. "Do you honestly think this man is going to let you beat him, fair and square? You know as well as I do he's a thief and a cheat."

"Hey, you better have some proof to back those claims up." Virgil stood up from the table to face the sheriff.

"Oh, I've got the proof. I've got enough people willing to speak up against you. And even if I didn't, I've had my friend here watching you as you played the last couple of hands against Brooks."

A man stepped out from the shadows behind Virgil. Brooks creased his eyebrows together and stood up slowly as he looked back at his friend.

"Mind telling me what's going on, Lewis?"

The man he didn't recognize stepped forward with his hand out to shake his. "My name's Harrison Winchester. Reformed scoundrel and Lewis's friend from way back." The man had a wide grin that covered his face.

Brooks shook the man's hand, then turned to look at Lewis, waiting for an explanation.

"I wasn't about to send you down here on your own. You may believe you're invincible but I'm not that stupid. I've heard too many tales about Virgil here to let myself believe he'd play fair. And I knew if you somehow did win, he wasn't letting you walk away alive."

"You don't know nothin' about me," Virgil hissed.

"That's where you're wrong, Virgil. See, I've

been standing behind you the whole time watching you play Brooks here." Harrison moved back to face Virgil.

"Like I said, I'm a reformed scoundrel myself and I've played a hand or two of cards. I also know how to cheat, just the same as you. I've been watching you and I don't think you want me to ask you to lift your sleeves right now, do you?"

Virgil moved faster than anyone expected for a man his age. Before they had a chance to react, he'd slammed into Harrison, hollering as he knocked him to the ground.

Lewis grabbed him and pulled him up by the scruff of his shirt. As he did, cards fell out of Virgil's sleeves, landing on the ground at his feet.

Lewis threw the man toward Harrison, who promptly cuffed his hands together and dragged him outside.

"Sorry to take your moment away from you, Brooks, but I thought you'd want to know what I had to tell you."

Brooks still stood at the table, shaking with anger. He didn't know who he was the angrier at, Virgil for cheating, Lewis for taking away his chance to beat the man at his own game, or himself for letting himself be so consumed with the need for revenge.

And now it was all for nothing.

"Fiona's left."

His head snapped around at the words. "What do you mean? Where did she go?

"She went home. She signed the annulment papers for you first."

The room around him started to spin as he realized he'd lost the woman he'd fallen in love with, all because he had a score to settle with a man who'd never have let him win anyway.

CHAPTER 24

The sound of the horse's hooves thundered beneath him as he raced over the ground.

Fiona had a few hours lead on him but he also knew the train she'd gotten on had to make a stop just outside St. Louis. He had the advantage of being able to go across the open fields and country that would get him there faster.

He just hoped it would be in time.

Brooks didn't know what time the train would leave in the morning but he knew he had to be there before it did.

He needed to hear her say it herself, that she wanted to go home. And that she wasn't willing to stay and give him a chance. He wanted her to say it to his face and then he'd let her go.

Not that he'd blame her if she did say it. He'd made a mess of things right from the beginning.

And now she was on a train headed as far away from him as she could get.

If he was a smart man, he'd let her go.

But he'd never been accused of being smart.

Ignoring the pain in his side as he roared across the countryside, all he could think about was that no matter what had happened with Virgil today, none of it mattered if he didn't have Fiona with him.

He knew she deserved better than the likes of him but he also knew he had to see her at least one more time.

He was still a betting man and he was gambling on her being willing to take a chance on him.

❧

SHE HEARD the steam let go from the train as they prepared to board. She held tightly to the bag she'd carried with her from London. Now, it held everything she'd come out with, plus one shirt that belonged to Brooks. As she'd packed, she couldn't bear the thought of leaving without something that was his.

The conductor came over, taking her ticket and punching it, then he pointed to the door where she could board.

"Fiona!"

Her heart leaped as she imagined she could hear

Brooks' voice above the sounds of the train as it prepared to leave.

As she moved to the door, placing her foot on the first step, she thought she *could* hear her name being called again. Turning to the sound, she dropped her bag on the ground when she saw Brooks storming up the platform on his horse, the dust swirling around him as he jumped from the animal before it had even stopped.

Her hand came up to her throat as she tried to make sense out of it. What was he doing all the way out here?

"Fiona, wait. Before you get on that train, you have to listen to what I've got to say."

"But, Brooks, what..." She couldn't get her words to come out. She looked at him in shock, realizing he was covered head to foot in dust and looked like he'd been riding for days.

"How did you find me?"

"You didn't think I was just going to let you leave that easily, did you?" He tried to wink but he winced in pain.

"You've rode all this way and now you've surely opened your wound up again!" She moved closer to move his jacket aside to check for blood.

He grabbed her hand, pulling her away from the open door of the train.

"It doesn't matter. Just listen to me. I haven't

ridden all night to find you, only to have you start fussing over the nick in my side."

If she wasn't still in shock, she would have raised her eyebrows at the comment. He still wouldn't admit it was more than a mere scrape and he could have been killed.

He was still holding her hand and as she stood there waiting for him to catch his breath, the train whistle blew. The conductor gave the last boarding call but she could only stand still, looking into his eyes. They begged her to give him a chance to say his piece.

But she knew if she did, she wouldn't be getting on the train today and she didn't know when the next one would be through. She didn't know if she could resist him if she stayed.

"It's your choice, Fiona. But I'm asking you to please, just give me a chance. I know I don't deserve it."

"Ma'am? Sorry to interrupt but the train's got a schedule to keep and we've got to leave." The friendly conductor came over and tapped her on her shoulder, handing her the bag she'd dropped by the door.

Brooks' eyes pleaded with her.

"I'm sorry, sir, I won't be going with you today." He nodded, looking back and forth between her and Brooks, seeming to understand.

She couldn't just walk away from him, not after everything he'd done for her.

Brooks let out a breath and she could feel the muscles in his arms relax as he pulled her into his arms.

"Fiona, I want you to stay with me. I want ours to be a real marriage, one made in love."

Once again, she tried to find the words she wanted to say. She'd never dreamed she could find someone who could love her for who she was. A tear escaped and made its way down her cheek.

He pulled back, holding her in front of him. "I'm sorry, Fiona, I didn't mean to make you cry. I know you deserve better than a man like me but I swear I will do my best now to be the man you need."

She shook her head. "Don't you understand, Brooks? You've always been the only man I needed. You are so much more than you ever believed of yourself and I'm so thankful you were there that day when I walked into that saloon. You saved me and you've done everything you could to help me ever since, never asking for anything from me. Can't you see that you're a better man than any of the men I've ever known?"

He swallowed hard as he looked down at her.

"I love you, Fiona. I'd be a happy man if you'd stay here. With me."

He reached up and wiped the tear from her cheek.

"I love you too, Brooks. And there's nowhere I'd rather be than with you."

With those words, he pulled her into his arms again and placed his lips softly on hers. He kissed her until the world around them started to spin. Somewhere in the distance, she heard the faint sound of the train leaving the station and people talking around them.

When he lifted his head, she opened her eyes and saw all the love she felt reflected back in his.

"Most of my life I thought I was meant to be gambling, sitting in those saloons, waiting to fix the wrongs from my past." He brought his thumb up and gently touched her lips. "Now, I know I was sent there to find the woman who would give me my future."

As he brought his lips back down to hers, she sent up a prayer of thanks that Brooks had been a gambling man, there to save her when he was needed.

And now she was ready to wager her life and love, on him.

SPECIAL SNEAK PEEK AT BOOK TWO: A DRIFTER'S FORTUNE

Available now for pre-order!

CHAPTER 1

"*Now that I've got you all gathered together, it'd be remiss of me not to mention that I'm not particularly happy you're even hearing these words. Because if you're all sitting there listening to my old friend Henry read this letter, it only means one thing—I'm lying in a hole somewhere with my feet pointed to heaven and a mouth full of dirt.*"

Harrison held back his laughter as he listened to the letter being read to the group gathered in the lone saloon in town. Only Elijah Chance could manage to say the words so eloquently, even in death.

"*You all know I was a bit of a betting man and I couldn't resist having a bit of fun now and then. It was also no secret I never found myself a woman to share my life with and have no kin to pass my fortune down to. I never stopped believing maybe a woman would have come*" *my way if I kept lookin', but I guess my tired old body had other plans.*

"So, I've gathered all of you, the men who live in this barren town of Romance, Kansas, together after you've laid me to rest. I have a proposition for any of you who'd like to take on the challenge.

"Women are scarce around here, that's no secret. Not many women want to live in a desolate town like this with nothing much to offer for luxuries and the thought of living on a ranch with some of the strangest creatures known to man would be enough to deter even the toughest of ladies.

"Here's the challenge, if you decide to take it. The first man who can get a woman out here to marry him will inherit my fortune. That includes all money and assets, including my beloved Last Chance Ranch.

"But, here's the catch... (You didn't think I'd make it easy on you, did you?) The woman must be a complete stranger to you and since we live almost smack dab in the middle of this great country of ours, she has to come from either the east or the west coast. Let's make her have to travel some to get here.

"How you get her here or convince her to marry you, is of no mind to me as long as you don't lie, cheat or do anything else illegal. And that means no abducting any woman against her will, Charlie."

Harrison and the rest of the men in the room turned their heads to grin at old Charlie Billings. Charlie wasn't the smartest man in these parts. He'd also been known to get himself in trouble now and then by bothering the women when he'd head into the much more exciting town of Abilene.

It was a running joke around town that the man would never find himself a woman without having to steal her away.

"You need to convince her to marry yo, and stay on the ranch with you. If she's stayed after a full six months without running for the hills, you've got yourself the title to the ranch. If she does decide to use her head and run as far away from here as she can get, then the race is on again."

His head started spinning as he realized the amount of fortune that was at stake here. Elijah Chance had a lot of money, more than most of them could likely even imagine. And the Last Chance Ranch he'd built from the ground up was a one-of-a-kind attraction that drew in even more money every year.

This wasn't a small settlement these men would be playing for. As Harrison looked around at the others, he noticed they all sat in shock at the opportunity that had been granted to them.

"In order to make sure everything is on the up and up, the wedding must be performed by Henry himself. He has to assure himself that the woman isn't being forced into anything without her consent, that the woman is unknown to the man, and that she will be treated fairly."

No one moved, no doubt considering how they

could convince any woman to come out to Romance. The name didn't reflect the town accurately at all and had only been named that by Elijah himself as he opened up the small settlement. He'd never married but always believed that romance, and love, was possible for anyone. He'd thought it would be quite funny to name the town after something completely out of character for the place.

He'd been an eccentric old man and Harrison was going to miss him. Even though he'd only worked on the ranch for a few weeks now, he'd gotten to spend a great deal of time with him and Elijah had a personality you didn't soon forget.

The truth was, the letter they were now being read by Elijah's oldest friend Henry, was no shock to him at all. He'd known the old man would make things fun and exciting right up until the end.

And, he always wanted to give everyone a fair and equal chance, including the animals he saved, giving them a second chance on the ranch he'd created to house them all. Over the years, he'd created quite a collection of misfit and wounded beasts who needed homes.

Now the ranch was an attraction that people came from all over to see.

He still had the usual animals that were expected on a ranch. In fact, he had one of the largest herds of cattle in Kansas. But his first love was the critters no one else wanted.

Harrison knew this was a huge opportunity. This was his chance to make his own fortune. He could end up bigger than the family who wouldn't accept him, never believing he was good enough to work in the family business or inherit any of the family fortune.

The Last Chance Ranch was his own chance for making his mark in the world, even if it was a bit off the beaten path.

It didn't matter. Elijah Chance had given him the same opportunity as the other men sitting in this room—to make that ranch his own.

All he had to do was find a woman, convince her to marry him, and move out to the middle of nowhere with a three-legged goat, a camel, a baby wolf and many other creatures that sent most women running the other way.

He was sure it couldn't really be that hard to do. He'd made his way from New Haven to Abilene by making impossible wagers that had men believing he was a fool and he'd always come out winning.

Looking up to the heavens, he let the old man know this was one bet he was willing to take.

CHAPTER 2

"**P**ut this on your eye and it will help stop some of the bruising." Patience gently placed the cold cloth on her brother's eye.

"*Shhh!* You know if they hear you in here, you'll just be in as much trouble as me. Just go back to your room. I'll be fine."

Patience clenched her teeth tightly as she looked at her brother sitting on the bed, holding the cloth on his eye. He didn't wear a shirt and the bruises from this beating stood out prominently, plus the scars from previous ones. She swallowed hard, wishing she could just get them away from here.

"Mark, you're my little brother. And if I want to risk taking a beating to help you, then that's my decision. Now turn around so I can tend to the marks on your back from the strap."

Her brother's small back showed large, fiery red welts all the way across. A sob escaped as she saw how much damage there was this time.

"I swear, Mark, I will get us away from here." Her voice trembled as she tried to carefully wash the skin and offer it some coolness from the water.

"I'm the man and I'll figure out how to get us away."

She had to smile at her brother's attempt at being the man he believed he already was. However, he was three years younger than her; he'd just had his fifteenth birthday.

He always took the beatings, though, even if something was her fault. He never let them lay a hand on her, stepping between them and drawing their attention to him. It broke her heart that he did it but she'd done it for him for years when he was younger, so she knew he was now trying to repay her for the times she'd suffered for him.

Their parents had died when they were young and they had been taken in by relatives. No one had ever really explained the family connection but they went by the last name of the couple who'd raised them. Daniel and Andrea Thompson weren't nice people but, as far as they knew, they were the only kin they had left.

Patience couldn't really remember their parents, only vague recollections of memories that weren't clear in her mind. She sometimes thought she could hear her ma's voice or start to see glimpses of her pa's face in her memory but they always seemed just out of her reach. She'd only been four years old when they'd died coming out on the trail to Oregon. Her brother had only been a baby, so he had no memories at all.

She couldn't remember being brought to these relatives but, apparently, they'd been brought there by a family on the wagon train. And since the day they'd arrived, they'd been little more than free labor. They'd never been shown any love and Patience couldn't understand what they'd ever done wrong to deserve the mistreatment they endured.

But she'd had enough this time.

They'd almost killed her brother and she wasn't going to put up with it anymore.

"I'm answering the advertisement, Mark. This is our way out. Nothing can be worse than what we're suffering at the hands of Daniel and Andrea."

She'd been looking at advertisements in a paper that were looking for women to be mail order brides. Most of the notices were from men out in the west, where women were scarce.

But she'd been searching for one that would be as far away from the Thompsons as they could get and she'd found one yesterday that seemed perfect. However, whenever she mentioned it to Mark, he'd get angry, insisting he'd find a way for them to get away.

He didn't want her being put at risk by marrying a stranger.

"There's no other way. And I'm not waiting for them to kill one of us. You're getting to an age where they expect you to do so much and because you're getting bigger, their beatings are getting more severe."

Her brother was still small for his age and she had no doubt it was because they were given just the minimum amount of food they needed to survive. Also, Mark always insisted she have her fill before he did.

"No way, Patience. I'm not letting you end up in an even worse place than we are now."

Mark's voice shook with anger and frustration as she dabbed at the wounds on his back with a cold cloth. She didn't care anymore if he was angry with her. He may be the man in his eyes but she was the oldest.

It was time for her to step up and save them before things got even worse.

When she got back to her own cot, she pulled the paper out from beneath her pillow. She read the words once more that she knew were meant for her to see.

"Wife wanted immediately. No time for correspondence. All matters will be taken care of for your transportation to Kansas from wherever you are. Searching for a woman who isn't afraid to work, not afraid of animals of

any kind, and who will be willing to be married upon arrival, under agreement of staying at least six months. You will be treated fairly and have all of your needs met by a handsome man with a kind disposition. Money will be sent for your ticket on reply."

It wasn't giving her much to go on and sounded odd after reading some of the other advertisements which were asking for certain traits in the woman. They also provided a bit more information about the groom-to-be. Most notices wanted to correspond first to see if they'd be a good match before any money was sent. Mark said it sounded like something wasn't quite right with it but Patience, somehow, felt it was their answer.

For all she knew, he could be an old codger with no teeth, hair or money but, at this point, she didn't care if he was lying. If he treated them with even a small amount of kindness, it would be more than they were getting here with the Thompsons. And, if it was really bad, it sounded like she was only bound to stay for six months.

Maybe she could even get so lucky and find he truly was handsome and kind. Maybe she might even find someone who she could love and who would love her in return.

Somehow, she didn't really believe that could be true.

She shook her head to clear the wishful thinking as she pulled out some paper and a pencil to reply.

AVAILABLE JANUARY 2022

ABOUT THE AUTHOR

USA Today Bestselling Author, Kay P. Dawson writes sweet western romance – the kind that leaves out all of the juicy details and immerses you in a true, heartfelt love story. Growing up pretending she was Laura Ingalls, she's always had a love for the old west and pioneer times. She believes in true love, and finding your happy ever after.

Happily married mom of two girls, Kay has always taught her children to follow their dreams. And, after a breast cancer diagnosis at the age of 39, she realized it was time to take her own advice. She had always wanted to write a book, and she decided that the someday she was waiting for was now.

She writes western historical, contemporary and time travel romance that all transport the reader to a time or place where true love always finds a way.

www.ingramcontent.com/pod-product-compliance
Lightning Source LLC
Chambersburg PA
CBHW011451170626
46816CB00009B/2624

* 9 7 8 1 6 3 9 7 7 0 8 0 9 *